SHERLOCK HOLMES

and

THE ELEMENT OF SURPRISE:

The Wormwood Scrubs Enigma

By J. Andrew Taylor

Paperback ISBN   9781780922683
ePub ISBN   9781780922690
PDF ISBN   9781780922706

Published in the UK by MX Publishing
335 Princess Park Manor, Royal Drive,
London, N11 3GX
www.mxpublishing.com

Cover design by www.staunch.com

"Grateful acknowledgment to the Conan Doyle Estate Ltd. for
permission to use the Sherlock Holmes characters created by the late
Sir Arthur Conan Doyle."

Map elements used by permission. Old Towns Books and Maps @
www.oldtowns.co.uk

Dedicated to my wife and children.

Thanks to my elder brother Stuart, who has been my "Mycroft" throughout this venture.

Special thanks to my niece Aleeya for being the first to read (and love) this book.

CHAPTER ONE

Having myself, been preoccupied with domestic concerns as well as a fledgling private practice, I had seen very little of my friend and one-time roommate Sherlock Holmes since clearing up the affair of The Red Headed League a month prior. I had assumed that these two reasons alone were to blame for our sporadic visits. Later, I learned from Holmes himself that, had I somehow found the time and occasion to call on him, he himself would probably not have been reached at our old quarters on Baker street, being there so seldom himself as of late.

Having also been both friend and comrade to Sherlock Holmes for nearly nine years, I had grown accustomed to his unannounced vanishings as well as to being made to wait until after the fact to know the reasons behind said vanishings. One such occasion occurred on the 2nd of November 1890. That morning, I received an urgent summons from one of my patients living very near Baker Street. It was not a difficult case after all, and by mid-morning, I found myself within walking distance of 221b. With a temperate morning, a blank appointment register and a sudden urge to check up on my friend, I made a slight course correction toward my old rooms.

I was just reaching for the bell to ring up Mrs. Hudson when suddenly, the door flew open and someone came careening through the door and bowled into me, nearly sending me hurling down the stairs.

"I say! What's all this then?" I demanded curtly, while trying to regain my legs.

A familiar face stood staring dumbfounded and ashamed back at me from under a crop of unkempt and disheveled hair.

"Please forgive me Doctor. I didn't expect….." Inspector Lestrade said, sheepishly while nursing a bruised shoulder.

Having regained my composure, as well as being

more curious than angry, I forced a smile and nodded my forgiveness. "Nor did I expect you Inspector. I came by to see about Holmes also. I assume he is in?"

"Not a chance. Blast him!" Lestrade almost shouted while glaring up at the sitting room window. "He's not been reachable for a fortnight. Mrs. Hudson either knows nothing of his whereabouts or is covering for him. Either way, I don't know when he shall return.

Looking me straight in the eyes, he asked, "Do you know where I can find him?"

"Inspector," I replied half-feigning disappointment, "The facts that I am here and have already asked you if he was in should have told you that I know no more than yourself."

To my utter surprise, I believe that I actually saw the man "deflate". He sighed heavily and stood there rubbing the uncharacteristic two days of growth on his chin. "I must apologize again Doctor. I've not been sleeping at all well lately and haven't been up to my mark these past weeks."

"I could prescribe something to help you rest." I

offered.

"No. Thank you all the same, but I cannot be hampered further by opiates."

"I understand. At least let me prescribe a glass of bingo from Holmes' Liqueur cabinet. I'm sure he wouldn't mind."

He was about to refuse when I stopped him by holding up my hand and saying, "Doctor's orders."

Smiling at this, he rang the bell. Mrs. Hudson opened the door and before seeing me, said to Lestrade, "I've told you Inspector.... Oh! Hello Doctor. I didn't know *he* was with you."

"It's quite alright Mrs. Hudson. I came by to see Holmes and ran into the Inspector at the door."

Lestrade saw the humor in this and chuckled under his breath.

"As I told *him,* Mr. Holmes isn't here. Hasn't been since a fortnight before all saints day."

"So I gather. Mrs. Hudson, I've walked some distance today and the old wound and I are shall we say, (here I patted my leg for sympathetic effect) in disagreement again. Do you think Holmes would mind his old roommate resting for a few minutes in his sitting room?"

A sly grin came over her round Scottish face. "Ack! Doctor. You know as well as I that Mr. Holmes still considers these rooms yours as well." She opened the door wider and stood aside. "Come through, I believe you know the way. You start a fire and I'll get some tea." She went off, humming to herself as if happy to have someone to care for in Holmes' stead.

I set to work at once. Being that the coal scuttle also contained Holmes' cigars, I temporarily moved the cheroots to get at the coal and piled a few lumps into the fireplace. I lit them and promptly I was, once again, sitting before a warm and inviting fire in that familiar old hearth at 221b Baker Street.

Mrs. Hudson came in with the tea and set it out for us. We drank it in relative silence until I noticed Lestrade eyeing Holmes' decanters of spirits. After filling my pipe from the Persian slipper and smoking in silence for a while, I got up and went to the spirit cabinet. "Brandy Inspector?"

"A flash of lightening if it's there." He answered a little too eagerly.

I poured myself a brandy and him his gin and returned to the fire.

Handing him his glass, I said. "Bite your name in on this glass and tell me what has you in such a state of agitation as to need Holmes so desperately."

"Don't misunderstand me Doctor." He said, recovering some of his usual ego. I've just come across a case that Mr. Holmes, being an amateur detective and all, may find useful in furthering his training."

I choked back a laugh. I lied and blamed it on Holmes' tobacco being stale.

"Mr. Holmes," he continued with a suspicious glance in my direction, "being well on his way to achieving notoriety in his hobby could be of some usefulness to the force; primarily now of all times."

He turned introspective at this and drained his glass in a single draught.

"What do you mean 'Primarily now'?" I inquired.

"As you recall Doctor," he began as he got up and

took the forgivable liberty of pouring himself a second glass, "The Metropolitan Police Force has grown to well over thirteen thousand men and the crown is moving us from Whitehall Place, into our new headquarters near the clock tower at Westminster."

"Of course. I had forgotten."

"You may have forgotten Doctor but I assure you, every hoodlum, every dinger picking pockets on Fleet Street and every filch in Greater London remembers, and they all seem to be taking advantage of the inescapable and predictable chaos that has been 'The Yard' during our lagging to our new roost by month's end."

Lestrade was becoming agitated again. He gulped the draught of his gin and shot a glance at the door. "Where *is* that man? I should have an all points search placed on *him* and have him brought in."

I chuckled and raised my glass of brandy toward him in an attempt to calm him some.

"Somehow," I replied, "I believe that if Holmes were to go to ground, neither Scotland Yard, nor even I, myself would know of his where-a-bouts." (*Little did I appreciate my own sooth-saying until almost four years later.*)

Lestrade saw the absurdity in his statement and conceded. "Of course, you are right Doctor. I'm just grateful that your friend is on our side of the dock."

"And all of London and most of the continent as well, Inspector." I added.

Finding myself intensely interested in hearing about this new case, yet feeling apprehensive about discussing it without Holmes present, I throttled my curiosity and moved the conversation toward more mundane affairs. We talked for half an hour in such a manner, then bid each other farewell and went our separate ways. I to my home and Lestrade (I presume) back to Whitehall.

As I exited onto Baker Street, I too looked back up at the now darkened window and wondered aloud, "Where have you gotten off to Holmes?"

CHAPTER TWO

Later that evening, while Mary and I were returning from enjoying the new Lutz & Sims musical *"Carmen up to Data"* at the Gaiety Theater, I hailed a brougham to take us from Aldwych, to our home in Kensington. Outside the theater, there was a long line of cabs all jostling for fares. These cabbies can be aggressive at times and we were forced to wait until some orderliness returned. Finally, a cab presented itself to us. I helped Mary into the cab, but before we could give our destination to the cabbie, the vehicle lurched forward and we found ourselves speeding down The Aldwych road; me hanging onto the exterior lamp and doorframe and Mary rolling topsy-turvy between the seats inside.

I shouted at the driver to stop and was answered by the imbecile cracking the whip even harder and sending us racing down the busy street at what I guessed after the fact, to be a breathtaking ten miles per hour. Thinking the cur to be a highwayman and fearing for our safety, I remembered my service revolver. I pulled the weapon out, preparing to crack his canister with the butt-end or to shoot him if necessary.

"Stop this cab at once man!" I yelled.

Receiving no response, I leveled the gun and aimed it at him.

"Pull to or I swear….."

"You wouldn't shoot your friend and savior would you Watson?"

Blinking as much in disbelief as because of the wind in my face, I peered at the cabman's face. The profile became familiar to me.

"Holmes!? I exclaimed. "What the deuce is this about?"

Reigning in the horses and pulling the cab to a stop on a side street off of The Strand, Holmes jumped down and removed what was his most convincing disguise yet.

Again I questioned my friend as to his motive for this outrageous and dangerous stunt.

He held up a finger and peered into the darkness of the night in the direction from which we had just come. I see you've brought your medical bag. "Take the cab home and see to Mrs. Watson, I will meet you there shortly and then all will be explained my old friend. He tilted his head past me into the cab. I do believe she has fainted." He added coldly.

A quarter of an hour later, the maid and I were nursing a much shaken Mary as she reclined on the settee in our parlor. Holmes arrived ten minutes later, but did well to keep a safe distance in a chair by the door. Mary did not dislike Holmes. On the contrary, she admired him greatly. Yet, at times, their relationship, where my involvement in his cases was concerned, could be somewhat strained. This particular exploit, I (as well as Holmes) could tell, had pushed her past her usually tolerant limits.

After a mild sedative and glass of port began to take effect, Mary dismissed the maid and then raised herself upon one elbow. "Mr. Holmes!?" She called over her shoulder without looking fully at him. "For the sake of your own honor, I hope that at least some of my John's talents at storytelling and, as you like to say, "embellishment" has rubbed off and that you can come up with a narrative sufficient to possibly explain your actions this evening." He was at her side in a flash. He stood with his wind tussled head bowed, dirty faced and wringing his cabbie's cap in front of him like a guilty schoolboy awaiting a thrashing from the head-master.

Neither I nor Mary had ever seen him thus, and Mary began giggling at the sight of the world's greatest consulting detective speechless and cowed. Holmes himself realized the absurdity and began to softly chuckle which quickly blossomed into a rare fit of genuine laughter. The three of us shared a friendly moment of jocularity which did much to heal at least the emotional wounds that Mary and I had been nursing.

After the laughter subsided, Holmes regained his usual poise, lit a pipe with Mary's permission and set out to explain the events leading up to that night's madcap coach ride.

"You must know Mrs. Watson," He began. "that I would never willingly injure either yourself or our dear Dr. Watson. Yet, tonight, as I was concluding my most recent case, I received an urgent note from one of those street Arabs we refer to as the 'Baker Street irregulars.' It stated that my newest enemy, having failed to locate me, had devised a plan to abduct yourself and your husband in order to "smoke me out". Here, he exhaled a large cloud from his pipe toward the ceiling to make the point. "Really John." He said turning to me. "I have frequently warned you not to take the first cab that offers itself to you. Tonight, I intercepted you and your wife before you entered that first cab and thus foiled your kidnapping."

I heard Mary gasp and I myself was slightly taken aback by Holmes' rare use of my Christian name and took it as proof as to the seriousness of the threat.

Mary finally faced Holmes, smiled and rose to strike a regal pose. "That is sufficient Mr. Holmes." She said. "I also know my John well enough to know that he will need a much more detailed account than that. But, as for myself....to bed. Good evening Sherlock and try not to keep John up too late please." She kissed the top of my head and turned toward the stairs.

Holmes rose and bowed. "As you wish Mrs. Watson. Good night."

We sat in silence a while watching the fire until I glanced at Holmes. He was in deep thought again and had a dire look about him.

"I must beg your forgiveness Watson for not making you privy to this case. I had no way of knowing that either you or your wife would be involved in such a way."

"Think no more of it Holmes." I replied.

"I would have informed you of course, but the case was of a somewhat personal nature."

"How is that?"

Holmes paused, and then looked at me. "Charles Bates."

I shrugged. "Beg pardon?"

Holmes rose to stand by the mantle. "Charles Bates was an old friend of my father. He is a country Squire in his mid-sixties, owns a large estate in Northhamptonshire and generally leads a quiet and reserved life. A month ago, I received a letter from him concerning the disappearance of his grandson William."

"Kidnapped?" I inquired.

"Nothing like it." He answered curtly. "Young William left home a month ago after a fierce quarrel between them and stormed off in a fit of anger; as young men who are approaching manhood are apt to do."

"I see."

"It seems that William ended up in the East End of London, having fallen in with a gang of pickpockets much like one that his grandfather, a young Charley Bates, then a London street Arab himself, was involved in some fifty years earlier under a man named Fagin. After some little investigation, and some help from 'The Baker Street Irregulars', I found and returned the wayward grandson. In doing so, I ran afoul of one Edger Cutler, the gang's leader. Cutler is a far more brutal man than Squire Bates' Fagin ever was and promptly tried to have me killed. Hence, my two week 'holiday'."

He removed a rumpled note from his breast pocket. "I received this note from the Irregulars after our…um…our ride this evening. They have informed me that the entire gang, including Edger Cutler, was apprehended while lying in wait for you along Aldwych road."

"Thank God!"

"All is well now my friend." Holmes said, throwing

the note into the fire. Holmes stood gazing into the blaze a moment, then chuckled under his breath. "This case is not without a turn of irony Watson."

"In what way Holmes?"

"As I have told you," he began, "the Baker Street Irregulars played a significant roll in locating the grandson of Squire Bates."

"Yes."

"Well," he continued. "'The Irregulars' were his brainchild."

"How is that?"

"Years ago, while I was at University, Squire Bates visited me and posed the idea of creating an 'unofficial police force' as a way of 'putting the street Arabs of London to a good use', as he put it."

"To amend the scenes of his own turbulent past as a pick pocketing street Arab."

"I suppose." Holmes agreed.

"Well." I said, as something of a segue. "Mrs. Hudson will be glad to hear that you're home."

"Undoubtedly."

"And poor Lestrade is in danger of a trip to Hanwell asylum due to your absence."

"Ha!" Holmes laughed and pounded the mantle with the palm of his hand. "An unintended bonus I assure you, Watson."

"Really Holmes!" I chuckled. "I occasionally question your ethics where that man is concerned."

"Fahh!" He exclaimed with a dismissive wave of his hand. "I'll send him a wire in the morning, inviting him to Baker Street for a late breakfast."

Holmes glanced at the clock on the mantle and then turned toward the door. He replaced the crumpled cabbie's cap on his head and tucked the riding crop under his arm. "Do you have plans for breakfast yourself Watson? I believe that Lestrade's newest puzzle will prove to be of interest to the both of us."

"How could you know that Holmes?" I asked.

"Because my dear fellow." He smiled. "They always are. Are they not?"

I bade my friend a good evening and watched as he disappeared into the wintry London night.

CHAPTER THREE

Late the next morning, I dropped in at Baker Street to find that Lestrade had not yet arrived. Holmes was still in his dressing robe, sitting on the settee amid a pile of crumpled pages from the morning's newspaper and looking very much like a bird perched in a paper nest.

"Good morning Holmes." I offered.

"Watson!" He exclaimed as he jumped up and rang for Mrs. Hudson. "Punctuality personified, as usual. No doubt a remnant of your military days."

"Precisely." I replied.

Holmes went to gaze out the front window. "Our friend Lestrade will not be far behind you." He said. "I've already had a telegram from him in reply to my invitation. Aha! Here he is now."

As if on cue, the bell rang and we heard Mrs. Hudson letting the detective in.

Moments later, the man himself entered the parlor and virtually threw his hat and coat on the rack in frustration.

"Mr. Holmes!" He exclaimed as if in chastisement.

"You are a cruel and malicious rouge. I really do believe that, in future, you should at the least inform either myself or Dr. Watson as to your whereabouts before you drop from the face of the Earth."

Holmes feigned hurt and smiled mischievously. "Really Inspector." He said. "I am repentant. Yet, I cannot believe that the sole reason for your visit is to remind me that crime takes no holiday in jolly olde London. What can I do for you inspector?"

Taking a seat and relaxing a bit, Lestrade drew a deep breath. "As well you know Mr. Holmes, Scotland Yard has recently moved to her new digs in Westminster."

"Of course." Holmes replied.

"Well," Lestrade continued, "For the most part, The Yard has been able to handle the expected upswing in petty crime and mischief."

"I had no doubt." Holmes assured him.

"Yet, there have been deeds done that are so grotesque and perplexing that even The Yard's best minds are finding it difficult to weave two threads together."

After a moment, Holmes relaxed into his chair,

drew his knees up to his chest and steepled his fingers on the bridge of his nose. Without looking up, Holmes said in a subdued tone, "Pray, Inspector, tell me the facts as you know them."

Lestrade stood and began pacing the floor in front of the hearth. "Mr. Holmes." He exhaled. "I understand you well enough to know that it has been a personal challenge for you to find the perfect 'locked room' scenario. You got damn close to finding such a case in '83 with Miss Helen Stoner and the Indian swamp adder. Before that it was the queer business of that man who was in such fear for his life that he hired a resident physician. What was his name?

"Blessington." I offered.

Oh yes, thank you Doctor Watson, 'Blessington'." Lestrade replied.

Holmes nodded his agreement, yet waved his hand in a 'get on with it' gesture.

Lestrade continued. "Mr. Holmes, I submit to you now, your locked room mystery in the English countryside in an open field blanketed with new-fallen virgin snow."

Here, Holmes sat bolt upright and I believe that I

actually saw my friend salivate. (At which, given the gravity of the crime, I am ashamed to confess I had to suppress a chuckle)

There was a knock on the parlor door and Mrs. Hudson entered with a large tray and after Lestrade and I cleared a space, she laid it out on the table.

"Thank you Mrs. Hudson." My friend said as the three of us sat down to break our fast.

"Please Inspector," Holmes urged. "Pray continue."

"You are familiar with Her Majesty's prison at Wormwood Scrubs in Hammersmith, near Shepherd's Bush?"

"Yes." Answered Holmes. "Though I have never been there myself, I know that it was built by convict labor according to a design by Sir Edmund Du Cane, isn't due to '*officially*' being completed until next year and yet already houses hundreds of prisoners."

"Yes. Mr. Holmes. That's the one." Lestrade answered, as if surprised by my friend's list of details.

(Here, I must interject to the reader that I myself had been to Wormwood Scrubs prison on two previous

22

occasions on medical matters involving inmates. Jhw) I said as much and urged Lestrade to continue.

"Well Doctor," Lestrade resumed. "Having been to The Scrubs yourself, you will remember that the entire area around the prison is still primarily a district of ancient forest and wasteland for some considerable distance."

I nodded my agreement.

"Four nights ago, on Halloween night to be exact, in the wee hours, it seems that a woodsman and his six year old daughter, who live in the forest south and west of the prison, came upon the body of a man dressed in the uniform of a prison Warder. The man had been decapitated. The guard lay in the centre of an open field bordered by the thick forest on the West, Wood Lane on the East and both the Wormholt and 'Old Oak' farms to the South, with roughly fifty meters of open, treeless land in any direction. The dead man's tracks in the snow indicated that he had come from the prison. According to the local constabulary, there are only three sets of tracks in the vicinity. One set belonged to the dead man; the other two belonging to the woodcutter and his sledge as he initially approached the scene to investigate."

Here Holmes held up a finder to interject. "What is the name of this woodsman, Inspector?"

"Mr. William Hollis, that's his name. He also testified that upon nearing the bloody scene, the body was still steaming from the neck stump where the man's head should have been."

Holmes sat up, lit his shabbiest clay pipe and threw the match into the coal scuttle. "I assume that you have arrested the woodsman then Inspector?"

"No." Lestrade answered curtly.

Holmes looked shocked at the negative answer. "Surely a decapitated victim and an ax wielding man should have been evidence circumstantial enough to at least *detain* the woodsman."

Here, Lestrade sat forward in his chair and focused his words at Holmes. "And there is your 'Locked Room' scenario Mr. Holmes. According to the report from the local constable, neither the woodsman's tracks nor the sledge ruts ever came nearer than ten meters of the dead man; much too far away for a man to decapitate someone with the swing of an ax. Besides, the woodsman has a solid alibi for the second beheading."

Both Holmes and I started.

"Second beheading?" Holmes nearly shouted.

"Yes." Lestrade answered with a sigh. "The next morning." Lestrade looked in my direction. "It was the very morning that you and I met here at Baker Street Doctor."

"Was this second murder similar to the first?" Holmes Inquired.

"Almost to the detail Mr. Holmes." Lestrade asserted. "The second victim was also a guard at the prison, traveling alone south of Wormwood Scrubs and had also been beheaded. This time, it was a Constable that discovered the body and swears that the victim's tracks were the only ones within a quarter mile. And, here is the thing that links the two crimes to the same culprit. In both cases, the dead men's heads are nowhere to be found."

"Extraordinary!" I exclaimed.

Holmes rubbed his hands together greedily. "Thank you Inspector. A first class retelling of the facts as of yet." He held up his finger, and paused in thought. "Tell me

Inspector. Has it snowed in Hammersmith since the first murder?"

Lestrade thought a moment. "No, it has not."

Holmes jumped up from his chair and turned toward his bedroom while removing his dressing coat. "Then there isn't a moment to lose before Mother Nature deals us a cruel blow by doing so and erasing the all-important evidence of the aforementioned tracks. "Watson!" He shouted from his room. "Are you keen for the hunt? How does your appointment register look?"

"Undoubtedly keen Holmes." I answered excitedly. "Though I will have to take a moment to send a telegram to Jackson to assume my daily rounds."

"Good old Jackson!" Holmes shouted. "What would I do without him?"

A few moments later, Holmes exited his room fully dressed and packed for travel. "We can make a brief stop at your home to allow you to inform Mrs. Watson and for you to pack as well."

On his way toward the door, Holmes paused as he passed me. In a low whisper, he said, "May I suggest that this case may require your service revolver Watson?"

"Without a doubt." I assured him.

CHAPTER FOUR

By five till eleven, the three of us were standing inside the Kensington High Street station awaiting the eleven o'clock train. Curiously, the entire arched interior, as well as the great glass ball chandeliers of the station had been decorated with banners and streamers in the colours of the Union Jack. I wondered at this in silence. Silence may be a deceitful word here due to the din and clamor of humanity that echoed loudly inside the cavernous building. The sounds of a hundred different conversations, labor and machinery filled my ears to capacity.

"Shall we go up to the pub in the arcade and indulge in a libation, gentlemen?" Holmes suggested over the noise and turned abruptly to walk up the stairs.

"But Holmes," I replied, "We will miss the train if we leave."

"Nothing of the sort Watson. It is most likely that our train will be somewhat tardy this morning."

"Poppycock!" Lestrade Interjected. "You may dally about at the pub if you wish Mr. Holmes, but I have a duty in Hammersmith and I will wait here for the eleven o'clock." He sat down on one of the benches on the middle platform.

I trustingly followed my friend up to "*The Pot and Kettle*" and drank a pint; all the while, I nervously watched the platform where Lestrade was now pacing back and forth. Presently, Holmes checked his watch, stood up, laid a few coins on the table and meandered back toward the platform. I checked my own timepiece as I followed and noted that it was coming up on quarter past the hour.

We took our places next to the Inspector and stood in silence until, after waiting until almost eleven twenty-five, Lestrade's patience and curiosity at last failed him.

"Where is that blasted train!?" He said, obviously frustrated. "And how the devil did you know that it was going to be late?"

"It is quite simple Inspector." Holmes answered, while indicating the station's decorations with his walking stick. "These ornamentations put me in mind of something that I had read earlier. According to this morning's *Times*, today is the day that *The City and South London Railway* is opening the first electrified railway in London. An inaugural ceremony, attended by The Prince of Whales himself, was held at the Stockwell station from ten-thirty to eleven and would have most likely caused the trains along these other lines to be subsequently delayed at least twenty minutes. These gaudy decorations are no doubt in honor of the day's festivities."

A hint of recall showed on Lestrade's face. "And so you left me here to stew did you?"

"Surely, a trained professional such as yourself had also realized the delay and just wasn't thirsty at the moment." Holmes said, his words dripping with sarcasm. I myself, coughed to cover a laugh.

"Yes. Of course." Lestrade mumbled and looked up again toward the banners. "Damned irresponsible."

"Quite so." Holmes agreed. "Yet even criminal investigations are, at various times, either aided or hampered by the march of mankind's industrial advancements Inspector. Shall we welcome and praise the former, yet wonder at and curse the latter?"

Holmes pointed his walking stick straight out in

front of him and pressed its brass tip to the track closest to us. "Ah! Here is the missing train now, if I don't miss my guess."

A few moments later, the train chugged into the station. The passenger cars had also been festooned with banners and streamers that flapped a staccato beat in the wind as if to applaud Holmes, and to further mock the Inspector.

"Damned irresponsible." Lestrade repeated tersely as we boarded the first class car.

I "coughed" again.

Once we had gained our seats and the train was under way, Holmes again fell into a contemplative mood.

"Where was our woodsman during the second murder Inspector?" Holmes asked. "What is his alibi then?"

The innkeeper at "*The Crook and Shears Inn*" in Shepherd's Bush about a mile south of the scene, will swear under oath that Mr. Hollis was in the pub the entire evening, and too far in his cups to have found even the front door; much less manage a nearly two mile hike to relieve a sober prison Warder of his noggin."

"And who vouches for the Innkeeper's story?" Holmes inquired.

"Two people do. One is the woodsman's daughter who was with her father that night also, being that he regularly takes her along to the inn."

I expressed disbelief in the form of a loud 'huff'. "He brought his young daughter out to trudge through the snow to a pub in the wee hours of the morning?"

The poor girl's mother died in childbirth, and so Mr. Hollis is wont to bring her in tow." Lestrade explained. "The little one told the Constable that, on the night of the second murder, she and her father stayed at the inn till morning's light."

"And the other person?" I asked.

"The Innkeeper's wife, feeling for the little girl, usually brings her up to their flat above the inn to play with their own children while her father drinks and then sleeps it off till morning. The lady will swear that she tucked the little girl into bed with her own little ones at nine o'clock p.m. and then, owing to maternal instinct, checked Mr.

Hollis' traveling condition every ten minutes throughout the three hours before and the two hour after the second murder, during which time, she says he didn't move a hair."

"That puts the second murder at around midnight then Inspector?" Holmes ventured.

"Very near twelve, yes." Lestrade clarified.

"And you mentioned that the first murder happened 'in the wee hours'?"

"Yes." Lestrade answered. "According to the prison doctor who has acted as coroner, it was within a half an hour on either side of two o'clock in the morning for that one."

Holmes sat back in his seat. "Very well. Thank you Inspector." He offered, after which, he became silent and turned to stare contemplatively out the compartment window. Lestrade and I kept each other company with talk of the facilities which comprised the "New Scotland Yard". We talked of other minutia and inert subjects for the rest of the trip.

As we disembarked at the station at Shepherd's Bush, a Constable stepped up to Lestrade, saluted smartly and introduced himself as Sergeant Quinn.

Lestrade returned the salute and indicated my friend and I. "This is Mr. Sherlock Holmes and his associate Doctor Watson. They are to be given the same access to the case as I myself have. Now, be a good man and take us to the scenes of the murders Quinn."

"As you wish, Sir." The man nodded, smiled at us and led us to a waiting coach.

"What about our bags then?" I inquired.

The Sergeant snapped to again and bowed. "I can have a man deliver them to…..where will you be staying gentlemen?"

Holmes spoke up. "If the good Constable would have them delivered to 'The Crook and Shears Inn', it would be most helpful."

"The Crook and Shears, Sir?" Quinn inquired. "Surely gentlemen of your status would much rather take rooms at a more accommodating establishment. Quinn raised his hand and pointed to a large building on the 'Nor Eastern corner. "Perhaps 'The Beaumont Arms' there across the street?"

I was about to agree vigorously to his suggestion of more refined rooms, when Holmes interrupted.

"'*The Crook and Shears*' will do nicely, thank you Sergeant." Holmes replied, not leaving the subject open for further discussion.

"Very good, sir." Quinn said, and walked over to a hay cart where a local farmer was sitting idly while his horses drank from a trough and made the arrangements to deliver our luggage.

CHAPTER FIVE

As Sergeant Quinn drove us out of the station in a dog cart, I was immediately struck by the smell of flowers in bloom. Being winter, the smell came as a pleasant surprise. The source of the aroma became clear as I noticed that we had passed '*Frithville Gardens*' with its many green houses. We turned west onto Uxbridge road and continued until turning north onto Bloemfontein road.

As we travelled northward out of Shepherd's Bush, I was astonished at how quickly the suburbs of the modern age yielded to vast tracts of farmland and woodland. We remained northbound on Bloemfontein Road and soon Quinn pointed out both the Wormholt and Old Oak farms as we passed them. These homesteads constitute the fringe of civilization in that nook of England. Beyond these farms, lay a combination of fields, meadows and ancient forests that stretched from Shepherd's Bush Northward, all the way to the dismal walls of Wormwood Scrubs prison itself.

After about the tenth part of a mile, Quinn reined in the mare with a whistle and pulled the trap to a stop next to a low stone wall that ran alongside the road to our right. The four of us exited the cart, hurdled the wall and trekked eastward over the snowbound and hibernating pasture and farmland. The early snowfall covered the countryside in a pristine and glistening blanket a foot thick and was so beautiful and peaceful that it very nearly caused me to forget the reason for our visit.

A hundred yards further, my reverie was replaced by horror as I saw a large crimson blemish on the snow that looked as if a huge glass of red wine had been spilled onto a pure white Afghani carpet by some careless giant. Next to the bloody mess, there could still be seen, an indentation of a man's body hollowed out in the snow. Between ourselves and the scene, there ran two parallel lines in the snow. Inside the ruts, there were footprints heading in a South Easterly direction. Holmes ran forward toward the scene, yet held up his hand to arrest us at an observable distance.

Holmes shouted back to Quinn. "I assume that these are the tracks left by Mr. Hollis' sledge?"

"Yes, Mr. Holmes." Quinn answered.

"And," Holmes continued, "I can see that Mr. Hollis is a very big man, wears furs and also has a large, but very obedient dog."

Quinn looked surprised. "It's just as you say Mr. Holmes! As true as Scripture! But how could you know all that from…."

Holmes dismissed Quinn's wonderings with a wave and continued on to the scene.

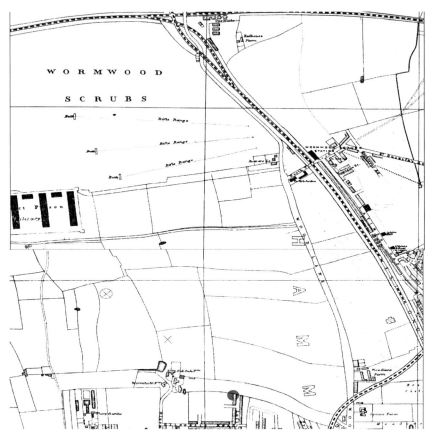

WORMWOOD SCRUBS PRISON, LONDON SOUTH TO SHEPHERD'S BUSH

Location of 1st murder   Location of 2nd murder   "The Crook & Shears" Inn

Had I not been familiar with the singular habits of my friend when the game is afoot, what Holmes did next would have been both perplexing and more than a little disturbing.   We watched as Holmes skirted the area, knelt down to study the blood soaked snow and then actually lay down in the dead man's imprint; staring up into the sky. Had a passerby happened to observe us, they may have thought Holmes merely resting during a country outing.

We then saw him jump up and begin walking a large circuit around the area.   Holmes then dropped to one knee, removed his magnifying glass from his breast pockct and peered intently at an apparently empty patch of snow. Jumping up again, he suddenly darted off in a 'nor easterly direction.   He called for us to follow, but with a large sweep of his arm, indicated to give the murder scene a wide berth.

After following him for a few hundred yards, he again dropped to one knee and studied another apparently empty snow patch with his glass.   After half a minute, Holmes got up and walked back toward the three of us.

Addressing Quinn, Holmes said, "I assume that the

additional footprints and wagon tracks were left by the men sent from the prison to fetch the body of the victim and were not here upon your initial inspection?"

"Yes, Mr. Holmes." Quinn replied.

Holmes rubbed his hands cheerfully, "And now Sergeant, on to the scene of the second murder if you please."

Quinn looked to Lestrade. The Inspector nodded his agreement. Quinn took out a notebook, looked around at the lay of the land and then pointed in a 'Nor Westerly direction. "This way gentlemen."

We trekked off after the sure-footed Sergeant for almost another three tenths of a mile. I had begun to feel the first twinges of pain in my leg when off in the distance, I perceived a scene very similar to the first. There again was a large crimson stain on the powdery carpet, with the definite impression of a human body in the snow next to it.

Holmes' approach to this second scene was identical to the first. Again, he held us at bay with his hand and approached the scene alone, in a wide circuit. We watched as he, as before, lay down in the indentation made by the unfortunate prison guard and stared skyward for half a minute. Holmes rose and continued marching around the scene in an ever widening arch until he again dropped to one knee and used his glass to study the snow.

Again, he shot off in a 'Nor Easterly direction until we saw him drop to his knees, glass in hand to peer at nothing.

"Aha!" Holmes shouted, jumping to his feet. "They are the very same!"

Holmes returned his glass to his breast pocket and walked back toward the rest of us.

"Where to now, Mr. Holmes?" Quinn inquired.

"I cannot speak for the Inspector or Doctor Watson here, but I myself have had enough of this crisp, clean country air for one day. I'm afraid that I've become accustom to the thick, smog-filled atmosphere of London. I propose that we adjourn to the inn, fill our bellies with stew and ale and our lungs with tobacco smoke in front of a roaring fire."

"As you wish, Sir." Quinn replied.

Half an hour later, we were scraping our boots and

doffing our coats in the main room of *"The Crook and Shears Inn"*. It was a low, smoke-filled room with dark wooden beams running along the ceiling. The walls were covered with oak paneling, shepherding implements (that gave testimony to both its name as well as the area's ancient trade heritage), and hunting trophies. The effect gave the place the feel more of a hunting lodge than a country inn. There were also a few gaming tables set throughout the room, occupied by some of the local men.

Walking up to the bar, we were greeted by Mr. Pinkerton, a heavyset man with large sideburns and a balding head.

"Welcome gentlemen, your bags were sent over from the station. I had the boy bring them up to your rooms. The Missus is up there now tidying things up." He looked confused for a moment and then inquired. "Will it be the three of you then? There were only two sets of bags sent over."

Lestrade spoke up. "I won't be staying. I've London business to attend to. I merely accompanied Mr. Holmes to set him upon the right path."

"A very perceptive observation, Mr. Pinkerton." Holmes said, as he signed the register.

"Only where my trade is concerned I'm sure Mr. Holmes. I've been an innkeeper too long to let something such as that get by me."

A female voice boomed from somewhere in the kitchen. "But ask him during a game of whist if he'd heard the Queen's guard march through the room, and he'll tell you he'd missed it all together."

Mr. Pinkerton's rotund belly shook as he laughed merrily. "A truer word has never been spoken my love. Gentlemen, my wife Mrs. Pinkerton."

Mrs. Pinkerton was a buxom lady with a round face, bright eyes and rosy cheeks, bookending a kind smile. She wore somewhat shabby clothes and a dirty apron, testifying to the myriad of chores which the running of an inn demands.

"Your rooms are ready gentlemen." Said she. "I have shepherd's pie and ale in the kitchen. Will you be dinning here, or would you like the boy to deliver it to your rooms?"

"Here will be fine, thank you." Holmes answered, reading my mind.

Mr. Pinkerton led us to a table in a cozy inglenook by the hearth, shooed away a couple of inebriated farmhands and cleared their detritus.

After delivering the promised dinner, Mrs. Pinkerton asked if there was anything else that we might require.

"The meal looks delicious, but if you would kindly point out Mr. Hollis it would be of some help to us." Holmes said, scanning the crowd expectantly.

"Hollis hasn't been in yet tonight Mr. Holmes." Mr. Pinkerton answered with a shake of his head. "Though I do expect he'll be here within the hour."

"Very good." Holmes said. "When he does arrive, would you be so kind as to make an introduction?"

Mr. Pinkerton nodded, smiled a nervous smile and then turned to go. He stopped short and timidly said. "Though, when he does get here, I would allow him a few pints before bothering him. He can be a mite rough of tongue before then."

"Well then, kindly ensure that his first few are charged to my account." Holmes offered.

The shepherd's pie was as appetizing as promised, but the ale was from a local brewer and was a wee bit weak for my tastes. After dinner, Holmes and I appropriated a couple of comfortable chairs by the fire and smoked in silence while we waited for our guest. I must admit that I dozed a few times before I felt Holmes' boney elbow in my ribs.

"Eh? What is it Holmes?"

Holmes nodded discreetly toward the door. "I believe that our woodsman has arrived."

I peered through sleepy eyes toward the entryway and saw a massive, dark shape filling the door from lintel to floor and from jamb to jamb. I had to blink twice to assure myself that I was not seeing visions. Hollis was a Goliath of a man. This woodcutter was very near seven feet tall with arms roughly the size of tree trunks themselves and the muscles of his chest jutted outward like the prow of a ship. On his head and face, he wore a wild mop of coal black curls and a beard that would have made Edward

Teach envious.

In almost circus-sideshow contrast, out from under his massive arm appeared a tiny slip of a girl with golden curls and cobalt blue eyes. He took her coat and she looked up at him beseechingly. He raised his enormous hand and patted her lovingly on her head. Receiving an approving nod from her father, she smiled and trotted off upstairs to (I presume) the Pinkerton's private quarters to find her playmates and the motherly landlady.

Hollis hung their coats on the hooks next to ours. With them, he hung the largest axe I had ever seen. As I contemplated the massive instrument, I could not help but imagine that axe and those arms lobbing off the heads of two unsuspecting prison guards not far north of there.

"Tut Tut, Watson!" Holmes scolded. "We mustn't make the man a murderer without facts."

"Well, yes but sheer the size of that......My blushes Holmes! You've read my mind again!"

"Merely because the thought had also occurred to me, old friend. Yet, we must remember that simply because a person is *able* to or has an *opportunity* to do something, does not intrinsically presuppose that they *did* the thing. It is a first-year mistake many a novice in my profession tend to make, many more in the official police force, I'm afraid."

"That particular naïve blunder has invaded the ranks of the news reporters as well. They would see a man hanged for the Whitechapel slayings simply because he happened to be a surgeon named 'Jack'."

Holmes took a long pull from his pipe and blew out a few rings toward the fire. "Sadly true, Watson. Sadly true today and even sadder still that it will probably be thus a hundred years hence."

I laughed at the thought, and ordered another glass of brandy. Mr. Pinkerton was just delivering the woodsman's first pint and, by the body language, I could tell that Pinkerton had informed Hollis that Holmes had picked up the tab. Hollis craned his neck in our direction and with a suspicious, yet honest smile upon his face, raised his glass to us. We returned the salute and let the man drink the autumn's chill from his bones in solitude.

After the man had imbibed his third glass of

Holmes' generosity, my friend signaled to Mr. Pinkerton that he wished an introduction. Pinkerton walked over, spoke a word or two to Hollis and then gave us a wave.

"Bill," he said to Hollis, "This is Mr. Sherlock Holmes. He and his associate are here at the request of Scotland Yard to investigate the prison guard business."

Hollis attempted to raise his giant frame up from the stool. He only made it half-way up and then sat back down with a thud. "Please forgive me gentlemen. Your kindness seems to have put me further into my cups than I had assumed."

"Think nothing of it, Mr. Hollis." Holmes said. "We only have a few questions if you don't mind."

"Alright then, have a chair and I'll try to satisfy your curiosity. Though, I've already told the Constable all about it."

"If you please, could you tell us the facts again as you know them?" I added.

Hollis took a deep draught of his ale and looked up toward the ceiling as if replaying it all in his mind's eye.

"'Twas on Halloween night, 'twas. My little girl

Agnes and me was coming over the fields on our way to the pub here; me for a drink, and Agnes to play and learn her letters from Mrs. Pinkerton."

"Learning letters? So, that is why you bring her all this way at night then?" I asked.

"Course it is. Her own sainted mother died bringing her into this world. I couldn't rightly leave her at the cabin all alone now could I? Besides, I aint got enough money for a proper schooling, and since Mrs. Pinkerton teaches her own young ones letters and numbers, I figured to ask her if Agnes could sit in on the lessons. Mrs. Pinkerton said she'd love to and so I bring her here after I sell the cords that I cut each day."

Holmes nodded understandingly. "Tell us about Halloween night, Mr. Hollis."

"Like I said, me and Agnes was coming across the field. I was pulling my sledge piled with Pinkerton's wood with Aggie and Cromwell riding on top under some furs."

"Excuse me." Holmes interjected. "Who is 'Cromwell'?"

"He's my mastiff Mr. Holmes. Had him since he

50

was a pup I have. A real Rum Buffer he is; keeps the wolves away while I'm chopping in the forest. Now, he's more horse than dog, really."

"Thank you, proceed." Holmes urged.

Hollis took another deep draught of ale and wiped the froth from his beard. "Suddenly, I noticed a dark something lying there in the snow just north of the Wormholt's farm. I got a feeling that something was amiss, so I left Agnes safely with Cromwell and went to see what it was. Before I got too near, I saw it was a man lying deader than a coffin nail. That's also when I saw that he had no head with steam rising from his neck. At first, being Samhain and all, I thought I was seeing the man's ghost coming out of his body to haunt us, so I stayed away. I heard Cromwell start barking, so I ran back to Agnes. The daft animal was barking at nothing that I could see. I calmed him and came on here to the pub."

"I see." said Holmes. Did you know the dead man Mr. Hollis?"

"Not at the time, being he didn't have a head and all. It was only later I found out it was Jenkins after Quinn told me."

"Did you know Jenkins personally?" Holmes continued.

"Of course I did. He used to come here most nights of the week."

"Do the prison guards usually come all that way at night?" Holmes probed.

"Sure they do. They come here to the 'Crook and Shears'. This ale is worth the walk across the Scrubs and the gaming tables are kinder than at any other boozing ken around here."

"Do you gamble Mr. Hollis?" Holmes asked.

"Not a bit of it Mr. Holmes! My money's too precious to me. I have little Aggie to think of and all. So I think one vice is plenty, eh what?" Hollis raised his tankard to indicate his drinking habit.

"Did you see anyone or anything else unusual that night; perhaps a farmer or other prison guards?" Holmes urged.

"Can't say as I did, Mr. Holmes. We came straight here and Pinkerton sent his boy to fetch Sergeant Quinn."

"There is one more thing Mr. Hollis," Holmes pressed. "May we have a word with your daughter about what she might or mightn't have seen that night?"

I saw Hollis tense at the request. "I don't see as how that could help."

"It is always good to get as many perspectives as possible from all persons involved; no matter the age." Holmes reasoned.

Hollis shrugged. "I'm still not sure. She's just a wee thing and I don't want to upset her any further over this business."

Holmes gave a sideways nod in my direction. "My friend here is a doctor with a fine bedside manner and a gentle hand; especially with children. You may accompany him as he interviews the young lady if you wish."

Hollis sized me up with his dark eyes, and thought it over. "I suppose that it couldn't hurt."

The three of us went upstairs to the Pinkerton's apartments. Hollis and I entered the little sitting room while Holmes stood vigil just inside the doorway. The little girl was sitting on the floor playing with some coloured letter blocks. When she saw her father, her cherubic face became alight with anticipation.

"Aggie, this is Doctor Watson." Hollis said gently. "He and his friend Mr. Holmes over there are helping the police and would like to ask you about what we saw the other night."

Just as quickly as it appeared, the smile faded from her face and was replaced by a look of unease. I stepped forward and sat down next to her on the floor. "Hello Agnes. Those are very pretty blocks. Which one is your favorite colour?

"Blue." She answered.

"I like blue also." I answered

I kept the conversation light and non-threatening for a minute or two. Then, at Mr. Hollis' nod of permission, I began the relevant line of questioning. "Agnes, can you tell us about the other night on the meadow? Did you see anyone or anything that might tell us who did the bad thing to the man?"

"It was very dark that night and Papa didn't let me

get close to the man that was hurt, so I didn't get to see anything." She looked at each of our faces in turn, and then blurted, "But I know who hurt him."

I turned to Holmes who now wore a look of amused surprise. He came closer and knelt down on one knee. "What do you think happened to the poor man, Agnes?" Holmes asked.

Ignoring Holmes completely, she looked up at me excitedly and blurted, "The wicked fairies did it, Doctor Watson."

"Do you mean something like Pookas?" I asked.

"Yes, Doctor." She answered ardently.

Trying to contain my incredulity, I pressed on. "Why do you say that? Did you hear something that night then, Agnes?"

"I heard the Pookas as they flew away. They flew over our sledge where I was sitting, so I don't think Papa heard them like I did; but Cromwell heard them and barked and barked. He chased them away."

"How can you be sure what you heard were fairies?"

"Because I heard their wings flapping and I heard them laughing and talking in squeaky fairy voices Doctor." She said, matter-of-factly as she started imitating the voices. She jumped up and began 'flying' around the room with outstretched arms making those little 'fairy' noises. I knew then that her childish mind had lost interest in our conversation.

At this, I saw Holmes turn and quietly exit the room.

I got up to follow Holmes when Hollis stopped me.

"I don't mean to impose Doctor Watson, but being that little Agnes and I live all alone and are of meager coffers, it's a rare thing for her to be seen by a Doctor. I was wondering if you could...."

"I would be my pleasure Mr. Hollis." I assured him.

"I could pay your fee over time of course."

I waved off his offer. "Let's just consider your help in this case payment in full."

"I'm obliged to you Sir."

"Think nothing more of it." I answered.

He summoned the little girl over and effortlessly

hoisted her up onto a side table. I examined a very healthy Agnes, accepted another round of thanks from Hollis, thanked them for their time as well and then went to join Holmes by the fire.

"Well Watson, what do you make of the girls testimony?" Holmes asked, as I sat down in a comfortable chair next to him.

"A child's fancy, I presume."

"Or, a child's misinterpretation of facts." Holmes countered.

"Either way, it seems that neither she nor her father can enlighten us further."

"So it would seem." Holmes agreed, as he lit his pipe again, stretched out his long legs toward the hearth and laced his fingers upon his chest. "So it would seem."

Holmes soon became quiet and withdrawn, so after enjoying another pipe myself, I left Holmes sitting by the fire and retired to my room for the night.

CHAPTER SIX

Early the next morning, after a hardy country breakfast, Holmes and I were met by Sergeant Quinn who drove us northward along Wood Lane to Wormwood Scrubs Prison. Having visited the prison previously (as I have stated), when we approached the ominous complex, I was struck anew by the juxtaposition of grandeur and gloom.

The architecture was at once both beautiful and hideous; much as when a seaman witnesses a thunderstorm appearing on the horizon. He is both in admiration of its splendor, and yet he is also filled with dread of its devastating power. Likewise, I was filled with both awe and dread when the magnificent edifice appeared upon the horizon.

The nearer we came to the prison, the size and scope of the place became more apparent. The walls seemed to rise out of the earth and gradually filled our field of vision. The entire complex was circled round by walls eighteen feet tall. Turrets, chimneys and gigantic cell blocks could be seen rising above the walls. Quinn drove us Westward along Du Cane road until we reached the main gate. The gate itself was flanked on both sides by two large towers, each decorated midway from ground to pinnacle with circular reliefs of those revered prison reformers, John Howard and Elizabeth Frey.

Quinn drove us right up to the arched entryway just as the door opened and two men came out. Quinn introduced the first man to us as Colonel James Calhoun, the prison's Warden. Had Quinn not used the Warden's rank in the introduction, I would have known him for a veteran officer nonetheless. He stood, talked and wore his uniform with razor sharp military bearing and comportment. His mustache was immaculately trimmed in a way that, I must vainly admit, rivaled my own. The other man was his assistant, Mr. Stevens.

Colonel Calhoun was gracious, yet distracted by our presence. Presently, the reason for his distraction became clear. A paddy wagon came driving up to the main gate. The markings on the side of the wagon identified it as being from 'Mall House Asylum'. Suddenly, the gate opened and four guards exited, dragging a raving, half-naked man between them.

I found it difficult to understand the apparent lunatic, other than a few short words or phrases buried between incoherent shouting and wailing. As the guards strong-armed him past the three of us, I heard the man well enough.

"You don't understand!" He shouted. "I'm not him! Somehow that fiend has done this to me!"

Both Holmes and I were caught a bit off guard by the unexpected outburst. The Warden seemed to notice this and apologized, saying that the prison was in somewhat of an uproar over recent events.

"The doings of the past few days have taxed the resolve of everyone on staff here, Mr. Holmes. I pray that you will understand my predicament."

"Absolutely, Colonel. Yet, this type of thing couldn't be too far off the norm, could it?" Holmes guessed, pointing toward the wagon.

Warden Calhoun rubbed his chin and stared after the departing wagon. "Prisoners here at Wormwood Scrubs enjoy living conditions that are far superior to any other penal complex in England. Yet, there are a few prisoners now and again that find confinement too taxing on their mental fortitude. The ruddy strange part of it all is that, if a person is going to break down, we usually see it happen within the first few months of their imprisonment."

Holmes indicated the wagon, now just visible down Du Cane Road. "I take it from your comment, that this wasn't the case with this poor soul?"

"That convict in particular is named Alpheus Skinner and is one of England's most notorious safe crackers. He has been incarcerated here at The Scrubs for almost three years. He suddenly went raving mad a few days ago; necessitating a transfer to Mall House, for evaluation."

Holmes gave the Warden an incredulous look. "Three years you say? Are you certain of this Colonel?"

The Warden seemed offended by the question and rising to his full height, faced Holmes defiantly. "I am aware, Mr. Holmes, that you hold a rather low opinion of Scotland Yard, but I assure you that the manner in which I run my prison is above reproach and when I say that convict Skinner there has been here three years, it is just so!"

"My apologies, Colonel." Holmes replied, "I meant no offense or to impugn your proficiency Sir."

"I should hope not Mr. Holmes." The Warden

huffed; the healing salve of Holmes' words of contrition doing little to mend his wounded pride. He indicated his assistant. "Stevens here will be your escort and will introduce you to the Warder that was on duty the nights of the murders. Good day."

The Warden turned, not waiting for a reply and disappeared through the door. A few moments of awkward silence followed with the four of us staring at the door and each other.

Stevens thankfully broke the silence first. "Well, Mr. Holmes, shall we begin?"

We followed the assistant warden through the great doors, into the prison's heart. We walked through the gate house and into a beautiful courtyard garden that was centered amid four long buildings that housed cell blocks four stories high each. Between the gatehouse and the courtyard, there was a beautiful and very nearly complete French Romanesque chapel. Anticipating my question, Stevens waved his hand at the structure. "Quite a bit further along since your last visit eh Doctor?"

"Indeed." I answered. "It seems to be essentially

complete."

He pointed to either side of the structure. "Actually we are just finishing those walkways there on either side to allow the convicts access the chapel during services on Sundays without coming into contact with the civilian visitors."

He went on to explain that the local parish had provided funding for the project in return for a cessation of all death sentences at Wormwood Scrubs.

"Very impressive." Holmes said half-heartedly.

"And a necessary supplement to the rehabilitation of these poor souls, I'm sure." I added.

We continued across the little garden and into what was obviously a sort of guard barracks. We were ushered into an anteroom with a waiting area and a high counter that ran the width of the room. Behind the counter, a large guard stood at attention when he saw Mr. Stevens enter.

"At ease, Mr. Burt." Stevens instructed, while indicating Holmes and I. "These gentlemen are Mr. Holmes and Doctor Watson in from London to look into the deaths of Jenkins and Baldwin. Gentlemen, this is our newest warder, John Burt." We nodded a greeting and Stevens turned back to the desk. "Has Mr. Teague arrived yet Burt?"

"Yes Sir, he's in the office waiting for you, just as you asked." Burt answered, as he unlatched a gate to the left of the desk. "But he's not in the most amiable mood just now."

"Well done, Burt. Carry on then." Stevens said, as he led us through the gate and down a short hall.

We followed Stevens to a room at the far end of the hall. A lone warder was sitting at a small table in the center of the room. He snapped to as we entered.

"At ease." Stevens ordered and then introduced Holmes and myself. He introduced the tall, well-built man as Teague and then excused himself; leaving the room and closing the door behind him.

Holmes took a seat opposite the man. "Thank you for making yourself available Sir. I will try not to take up too much of your time."

Teague leaned back in his chair. "Too late for that now isn't it then?"

Holmes was unfazed and turned his full attention to Warder Teague. "Mr. Teague, how long did you know your fellow Warder Jenkins?"

"I'll tell you what I told Burt out there. I didn't have anything to do with this business!" Teague almost shouted.

"As far as I am aware, no one has accused you of any such thing Mr. Teague. Now, if you will simply answer a few questions, I'm sure that all will come out right with you." Holmes said in his most soothing tone. "Now, how long did you know Warder Jenkins?"

"I knew him long enough." Teague answered, his words laced with some malice.

"Long enough for what Mr. Teague?" Holmes inquired.

"Long enough to know that he was a swindling gambler who drank too much and had a habit of roughing up the canary birds that are locked up in here."

"You say that he was a professional card cheat?"

"Right you are Mr. Holmes. Jenkins was a regular drop that would frequent the pubs and hedge taverns 'round here to cheat the bumpkins out of their wages."

"Was he doing well, as far as you know?" Holmes asked.

"At the first he did; always flashing his winnings around under our noses and all. But after word got 'round that he was a gammoner, he couldn't get anyone to take a chance with him. He soon got mucked out and lost everything. He became a regular interloper and started hitting me and the other warders up for a kick now and again; even lent him a few quid myself, I did."

"How many people would you say Jenkins was indebted to then?"

"Five that I'm sure of, Mr. Holmes; but don't get me wrong; he soon made it right by us all."

"He eventually paid his debts then?" I inquired.

"Yes Doctor. Just a week ago, he comes in and settled all his accounts. He said he'd had a good run at the tables lately."

"And what of Mr. Baldwin?" Holmes asked. "What was your impression of him?"

"He was a good sort I suppose." Teague said, his face softening at the recollection. "He went to church every Sunday, had a wife, and a fair hoard of bantlings to care for."

"So Baldwin had quite a few children?"

"Four lads and four lasses all tolled." Teague said, breathing a sigh and shaking his head. "Too many for my taste and wage."

"I assume, being the same rank as Baldwin, your wages were the same also?"

"Yes."

"So, Baldwin would have been wanting for money often?"

"I suppose, though Baldwin was a proud man and wouldn't have considered asking the other warders for a kick, like Jenkins did."

Holmes sat back in his chair, deep in thought for a moment. Finally, he sat up. "Did you also notice any positive changes in Baldwin's finances recently?"

Teague considered the question. "Now that you mention it Mr. Holmes, I was standing tout over the convicts in the chapel two Sundays ago and in comes Baldwin with Francis and the kids in tow; every one of them sporting new clothes and new flyers on their feet."

"Do you know from whence the windfall came?" I asked.

"Can't be sure," Teague answered, "but the scuttlebutt was the he was on the take."

"From whom may I ask?" Holmes prodded.

"Never found out, being that he lost his head a few days later as well." Teague hung his head. "I feel poorly for Francis and the children. They'll have a rough go of it now that Baldwin is gone."

"Do you put much stock in the theory that both Jenkins and Baldwin may have both been morally compromised and therefore susceptible to either bribery or extortion?"

"I must admit that, given the recent events, it does seem likely Mr. Holmes." Teague asserted.

"One last question if you please." Holmes said. "Where you on duty on either Halloween night or the night following?"

"Yes I was."

"Did you see or hear anything unusual that night?"

Teague though a moment, looked nervously toward the door and then at us sheepishly. "Well, yes but I'm not sure that I should say on the record."

"I assure you Mr. Teague that no one here at the prison need be privy to anything which you divulge to us here. You may trust both Doctor Watson and I and know that your reputation is safe with us."

Teague studied both of our faces a moment; sizing up the weight of Holmes' guarantee.

Finally, his shoulders dropped and he seemed to relax into his chair. "Well, on Halloween night, I was on duty on the southern wall. It was at the end of my shift and my replacement was late in relieving me."

"Who was scheduled to replace you?" Holmes interrupted.

"It was Baldwin now that you mention it."

"Very good. But what did you see or hear on that particular night?"

"As I said, I was standing guard on the southern wall and had just lit my pipe. I suddenly became aware of a far off sound from somewhere above my head that at first

I took to be music. I looked up, but I could not see anything."

"What did the noise sound like, then?"

Again, Teague got that sheepish look on his face and balked at the question.

Teague sighed and shrugged. "Well, what I heard could be nothing but the shriek of the banshee herself. Set the hair on my head to standing up. I thought it was sent for me and that my time had come. Of course, the next day, I knew she had done for Jenkins instead." Teague said, holding up a finger.

"Please describe the sound." Holmes urged.

"It was a long, high, wail of a sound. Not quite like a woman, but being that it killed Jenkins, it couldn't be anything else now could it?"

Holmes rose and opened the door. "Thank you for your candid answers, Mr. Teague. You may return to your post."

As Teague left, Stevens reentered the room.

"Well, Mr. Holmes, if we are done here, where would you like to go next?"

"To the morgue if you please." Holmes answered.

We continued on to the infirmary. There I was greeted by the familiar face of Doctor Phineas Brahms. We had become acquainted during one of my previous trips to the prison. He was dressed in a frock coat and apron. His graying hair was unkempt and stood out higgledy-piggledy from his head in all directions.

"Well, if it isn't John Watson himself!" Brahms exclaimed, while shaking my hand vigorously.

"Good to see you again Doctor." I said. "This is Sherlock Holmes. As I'm sure you are aware, Scotland Yard has requested that he look into the murders of your guards."

"I will assist in any way that I can of course." Doctor Brahms assured us.

"May we see the bodies of the victims Doctor?" Holmes asked.

"Certainly, this way if you please, gentlemen." The Doctor said, as he led us down into the basement of the building to the morgue.

Before entering the autopsy room, we took the

precaution of dabbing some eucalyptus oil under our noses to mask the stench associated with the decomposition of flesh. The Doctor entered first and lit the lamps in the room. It was a large rectangular chamber with four tables set evenly apart to allow ample working space between them.

On the two tables furthest from the door, the bodies of the unfortunate men lay, each covered with a large white sheet. Doctor Brahms led us to the nearest one and uncovered the body.

"This is Jenkins, the first victim." He said. "The other man was Baldwin."

We made our way to the first table. The body of the man lay nude upon the table with the arms folded across the chest.

Holmes looked to me and indicated that he wished me to examine the bodies. He, on the other hand, began peering around the room in search of something else. I made a cursory examination of both victims. On both, I noted that no torso incision had been made since the cause of death was so graphically obvious. As reported, the men's heads had been removed in a clean and sharp fashion that left no signs of ripping or tearing of the skin, muscle or bone of the neck. It seemed to me that even the most skilled of surgeons could not have made a cleaner cut, short of using a guillotine.

"Where are the men's clothing Doctor?" Holmes asked.

"There, in the cabinet, Mr. Holmes." The Doctor replied, pointing to a metal wardrobe opposite the door.

Holmes let out a frustrated sigh as he removed a bundle of uniforms that had been crammed together in a canvas laundry bag.

The Doctor, realizing why Holmes was perturbed, quickly spoke up. "I suppose that I should have kept them separated, but I was so focused on the task of preparing the bodies that I overlooked that detail."

"I suppose that we could measure the bodies to see which uniform belonged to whom, eh Holmes?" I suggested.

"Thank you Watson, but that won't be necessary. It is simply a matter of distinguishing them by the insignia of their ranks. Can you recall which man was senior, Doctor?"

Brahms thought a moment and then answered, "Jenkins was higher in rank."

"So," said Holmes, as he removed an overcoat and laid it on the table next to Jenkins. "The uniform with more chevrons belongs to Jenkins here. And, as Baldwin's coat has been regularly starched and pressed with creases and pleats, I deduce that the well-kept trousers also belonged to him."

Holmes turned back to the wardrobe and removed two pairs of shoes. "Now, as to the shoes." He said.

I studied the feet of both bodies. I made some quick measurements and turned to Holmes. "Both men seem to have worn the same sized shoes Holmes."

He began to examine in turn, the hands of each corpse. Having done so, he looked up at me. "As a general rule Watson, a person's favored foot is on the same side as their favored hand. I see here by the callouses on the index finger and thumb, that Jenkins here was right handed." Holmes turned to the other table and after examining the hands of the second man, said, "Baldwin however, apparently favored the left."

Holmes then returned to the shoes and after pairing them up, turned them over and examined the soles of each pair. "Here Watson, do you see? The scuff marks and wear patterns on the tread give evidence that the owner of *this* pair favored his left foot over his right." He laid the shoes on the table next to the second body. "These, therefore belonged to Baldwin; while this other pair were worn by the right handed Jenkins here."

Holmes removed his magnification glass from the breast pocket of his coat and, beginning with Baldwin's clothes examined the uniforms with intense single-mindedness. I knew better than to disturb him, so I returned to my examination of the two corpses. After some ten minutes or so, Holmes once again turned Jenkins' shoes over in his hand and began to examine them with his glass. As he did so, a small piece of paper fell out of one of the shoes and fluttered to the floor at Holmes' feet. "Ho! What do we have here then?" Holmes exclaimed, bending over to pick it up.

The note paper had been folded double and was somewhat wrinkled. Holmes unfolded the note and studied it for a moment. "It is written in a man's hand on common foolscap and seems to have been written hastily. See here? Observe how the paper is smeared, having been folded before the ink had dried."

"Let us see what Jenkins here thought so important as to have secreted it in his shoe." Holmes suggested and passed the note over to me to read aloud.

It ran thus:

"Lockyer was correct

Ramsay, University College, London

He will get the job done nicely.

Kober won't budge. Convince him"

A.S.

"This is most fortunate indeed gentlemen." Holmes said with a gleam in his eye. "It appears that Jenkins here has spoken to us from 'the great beyond', as it were."

"Who are these men mentioned in the note Holmes?" I asked. "Do you know them?"

Holmes studied the note again and with a nod, he folded the paper and put it in his pocket.

"These men Lockyer and Kober I don't recognize. But as for this 'Ramsay', the author of this note has seen fit to supply an address: 'University College, London'. Being somewhat of an amateur student of chemistry myself, *University College, London*' tells me that this Ramsay could be none other than William Ramsay, the preeminent leader in the field of chemistry. But what 'job' the author asserts that Ramsay will 'do nicely' is, as of yet, unknown. I believe that a visit to the University in Bloomsbury is in order, Watson."

CHAPTER SEVEN

We left the prison and Quinn drove us to the Wormwood Scrubs rail station. As we stood on the platform, Quinn turned to Holmes.

"Is there anything that I might do while you are away Mr. Holmes?"

"As a matter of fact, there is still the question of Warder Baldwin's sudden windfall. After all, given the benefit of the doubt, there may be a perfectly mundane reason for it. It would be of some value if you interviewed Mrs. Baldwin regarding this matter."

"As you wish, Sir. Where may I send a telegram as to the reply?"

"We will be at University College for most of the afternoon." Holmes replied, as we boarded the train.

We rode in silence; Holmes sitting and staring out at the scenery and me dozing across from him in the compartment. Soon, we disembarked at Euston station, very near Holmes' old lodgings on Montague Street. A quick walk found us in Gower Street, admiring the architecture of the venerable institution.

We crossed the quadrangle, climbed the steps and entered the building through the colossal Greek portico. We inquired as to the location of the administrative office from a group of female students and were directed to a chamber just on the opposite side of the rotunda. We entered, introduced ourselves and inquired if Professor Ramsay were available. We were escorted through the halls of the school to the Department of Inorganic Chemistry of which, Holmes noted, Ramsay had served as Chairman for the previous three years.

We were asked to wait in the foyer of the Professor's offices until he returned from a lecture. As we waited, I could see into the laboratory and observed that it was filled with beakers, test tubes, hoses, and gas burners. The assemblage obviously included the most advanced equipment of its type. It dwarfed Holmes' chemistry table back at Baker Street in comparison. I glanced over at Holmes and, unaccustomed as I was to seeing Holmes display his emotions, was surprised to see him eyeing the apparatuses with a brazen look of covetousness.

We did not have to wait long before Ramsay entered the office. As he chatted with his secretary, I noted that the man was much taller and thinner than most of *my* Professors at medical school had been. He was a man in his mid-thirties, was at least as tall and gangly as Holmes himself and he wore a goatee that came to a distinct point at his chin. The impression was one of unmistakable genius and unquestionable authority. He then walked over and greeted us both enthusiastically.

"Mr. Sherlock Holmes I presume." He said, in a thick Scottish brogue, while shaking my friend's hand vigorously. "'This is indeed a bonny surprise, Sir.

"The pleasure is mine, Professor." Holmes replied and pointed to me. "This is my friend and colleague Doctor

Watson."

"A pleasure to meet the both of you, to be sure." He stood, gazing at Holmes as if sizing him up to his reputation. "Mr. Holmes, I must confess that since reading your treatise on '*The practical analysis of oxides in criminal investigation*', and having also read of your exploits in *The Strand*, I have desired greatly to make your acquaintance."

"My blushes Professor." Holmes said. "That paper was merely a study on the subject of rust. You make too much of a trifle."

"On the contrary, Mr. Holmes. You see, I myself have also recently published papers on oxides. Though they are merely theoretical in nature, the difference is that, here at University, we academics usually deal only with the *theory* of our discoveries. You, on the other hand, have taken our theories, as well as having developed your own and have put them to *practical* use beyond the walls of the laboratory. And so, I must confess to the charge of envy." Here, he looked around the laboratory and sighed. "Would that I could break free of the gilded cage that I've built and ply your trade myself."

"I find myself humbled Professor." Holmes said. "And yet, there may be a way for you to do so; at least vicariously."

A smile crossed his face and a fire leapt into the Professor's eyes. "I would be delighted."

Ramsay led us into a sitting room next to the laboratory and offered us two chairs opposite a settee which he claimed for himself.

Holmes gave an abbreviated account of the singular events thus far and ended by removing the note found in Jenkins' shoe.

"A minor 'foot-note' in the story; as one might say." The Professor quipped.

I confess that I laughed loudly at the pun; though Holmes merely smiled briefly.

"Forgive me Mr. Holmes." Ramsay said contritely. "Go on please."

Holmes read the note aloud and then handed it over to the Professor. "Do the other names on the note mean anything to you Professor?" Holmes asked.

Ramsay stared at the note, with a look of bewilderment upon his face. "The only 'Lockyer' that I know of is Sir James Norman Lockyer, but he is only a harmless astronomer. They could not possibly be referring to him."

"And the name Kober?"

"I have never heard that name Mr. Holmes." He handed the note back to Holmes who then pointed to Ramsay's own name and the allusion to a 'job' that Ramsay would 'do nicely'.

"Have you any thought as to what 'job' the author might be implying that you would do Professor?"

Again, Ramsay looked bewildered. "I haven't the foggiest Mr. Holmes. No one has contacted me in regards to any endeavor that might require my.....wait a moment....There may be something."

Suddenly, the Professor fairly jumped from the settee and entered a small office adjacent to the sitting room. He returned a moment later holding a letter in his hands. "I have only just received this in yesterday's post." He opened the envelope and handed Holmes the letter.

Holmes read through the correspondence eagerly.

"In short," Ramsay explained, "it is a letter from a fledgling engineering company; '*Industrial and Engineering Trust Ltd.*', I believe the name is. In the letter, they request that I review and then professionally endorse their invention of a secret process that they claim, can extract gold from common sea water."

"Do you believe that it is a plausible enterprise?"

The Professor shrugged. "As I have said, I have only just received the letter. It could take months or years to study all of the formulae thoroughly enough as to justify risking my professional reputation with an endorsement."

"I believe, Professor, that this could very well be the 'job' that *our* note mentions." Holmes observed.

"Do you really think so?"

"It may be that someone is planning to steal any formulae that you may become privy to concerning this company's endeavors." Holmes speculated

"I suppose that it *is* possible." Ramsay agreed.

"If so," Holmes added, "it may be that your life is in grave danger, Professor."

Ramsay's face obviously registered apprehension. "What do you think I should do Mr. Holmes?"

Holmes thought for a moment, stood up and handed the letter back to Ramsay. "First of all, you will need to secure this letter in the safest of places. Next, I will wire Scotland Yard to send 'round two, plain clothed Constables, to offer protection until this business is worked out."

"Do you think that it will be enough?" Ramsay asked.

"Undoubtedly so." Holmes replied, "And you may also contact Inspector Lestrade on my behalf, day or night, if you feel the need of anything further."

"Thank you gentlemen." Ramsay said, as he stood to shake our hands in turn. "Though, when I had wished for some excitement in my life, this was not what I had imagined."

We left Ramsay's office after offering a few more assurances, and he seemed confident enough. We made our way back to the main entrance of the University. As we were walking down the front steps, a young Page met us with a telegram from Quinn.

Holmes read it aloud.

*"Baldwin gave wife no explanation for money
Windfall still a mystery."*

"What do you make of it Holmes?" I asked. "What does it mean?"

"It means, my dear Watson, that both Jenkins and Baldwin made deals with the devil. And it is our job to exorcise that devil."

Holmes turned, gave the Page a sovereign and sent him off with a telegram of his own to Scotland Yard; making the arrangements for Professor Ramsay's protection. At the foot of the steps, Holmes turned to me and pointed southward down Gower Street.

"Well Watson, providence has placed us to within blocks of *'The Alpha Inn'*. What do you say to a proper dinner here in London before returning to Shepherd's Bush?"

"Capital idea, Holmes!" I answered a little too enthusiastically. "Lead on!"

After a wonderfully civilized meal, Holmes and I

returned to the little inn on the edge of the wilds of upper Hammersmith; and to the phantom head-hunter that dwelt there.

CHAPTER EIGHT

Well past eleven o'clock on the evening of the 5th, after only a few hours' sleep, Holmes knocked on the door to my room at the '*Crook and Shears*' and entered. He was carrying my coat, medical bag and walking stick.

"Fancy an evening stroll Watson?"

"At this hour, Holmes!?" I challenged.

"Being that the murders occurred at night, the sights and sounds of the surrounding area are sure to have been different from that which we observed during the bright, sunny day on which we first were there."

"Most assuredly." I agreed groggily.

"My intention is to observe the scenes under the same conditions as existed on those nights."

"I see." I lied, yet I dressed and grabbed my things all the same and headed for the door.

A quarter of an hour later, we were heading north from the inn and just passing to the East of the Old Oak Farm. There was no moon and the darkness was an almost palpable curtain to my eyes. Both Holmes and I carried lanterns which we had borrowed from Mr. Pinkerton prior to leaving. As we entered the expanse of The Scrubs, I noticed a curious, haze of smoke hanging low to the ground which rolled and undulated in the soft breeze like some shapeless, living creature. The nebulous smog rolled between the bare trees far off to the west, hugged the contours of the open field and hove around our feet.

My first thought was that there was either a forest or grass fire near to our position. As we marched on through the smoke, a strange sound began to pluck at the edges of my hearing. The sound glided nimbly on the air and reverberated between the trees to the west. I, at first, believed that I was merely imagining the peculiar noise. To my wonder and dread, I began to recognize the sound as that of children chanting and singing.

Stranger still, the distant voices seemed to be emanating from more than one direction. They were coming, at first, from the surrounding woods, then from the direction of the farmhouses, then again from the direction of the prison. I could now hear a few words of the ethereal mantra becoming distinct.

"Remember……..Treason……Plot"

My flesh crawled and a chill crept up my spine as the children's voices became louder and more pronounced. The memory of little Agnes' allegation that evil fairies dwelt in The Scrubs as well as Teague's story of banshees flooded my mind. Finally, being able to tolerate no more of it, I stopped and attempted to locate the source. As I stood there, I noticed that in all directions, I could now see tiny points of light, like so many will-o'-the-wisps flickering in the blackness of the night. I glanced over at Holmes but, if he was also seeing and hearing it, his stoic expression gave no clue. This added to my apprehension that I alone was hearing the spectral choir.

"Do you hear it Holmes?" I finally asked.

"The children singing you mean, Watson? Yes, of course."

I breathed a sigh of relief. "Well, you could have at least said something man! I thought that I was going barmy there for a moment."

Holmes chuckled.

"What do you make of it then?" I queried.

"It is November fifth, Watson. Bonfire day."

{To my readers outside of Briton, I feel that I must quickly explain. As our American cousins may or may not be aware, November Fifth is Bonfire Night or "Guy Fawkes Night" and commemorates the foiling of an assassination attempt upon King James I known as the gunpowder plot of 1605. Guy Fawkes was arrested as he stood guard over a load of gunpowder in the basement of Parliament in London. Every year on the night of November fifth, children here in Britain light bonfires, eat treats and sing a well-known chant:

Remember, remember the fifth of November
Gunpowder, treason and plot
I see no reason why gunpowder treason
Should ever be forgot

Guy Fawkes, Guy Fawkes, 'twas his intent
To blow up the King and the Parliament

Three score barrels of powder below
Poor old England to overthrow
By God's providence he was catched
With a dark lantern and burning match
Holloa boys, holloa boys
God save the King!
Hip hip hooray!
Hip hip hooray!

JHW}

"Of course! I had forgotten completely!" I replied. "Right sinister sounding on a night and in a place such as this."

"I suppose."

We walked on until at last we came once again to the spot of the first murder. Unlike on the occasion of our first visit, Holmes seemed more interested in the feel of the location than with forensic details. Although he did, as before, lie down in the shadow of the dead man and look toward the sky. He turned down his lamp and signaled for me to do likewise. I complied and he lay there for five minutes or so, listening and watching.

"Pardon my curiosity Holmes" I finally whispered, "but what, pray, are you searching for?"

He stood up and brushed the snow from his clothes. "Fairies, Watson. Fairies." He answered and began walking South West of the scene.

Feeling to be the victim of Holmes' singular sense of humor, I protested. "You can't be serious Holmes! Fairies? Surely, you can't mean to say that you believe the little girl's story?"

"Absolutely." Came his unexpected reply.

"Now, I do feel the butt of a joke." I said, wounded.

"I believe the *facts* of her story Watson, but not her childish interpretation." He said in an apologetic tone. "Obviously, there was something here the night that both Hollis and his daughter saw as they were walking across The Scrubs; something that stirred her innocent mind to invent Fairy-folk as she tried to make sense of it."

"It could have been entirely her imagination, triggered by her father's obvious anxiety." I argued.

"Not so, Watson. It must have been something

corporeal and tangible, as evidenced by the dog Cromwell's reaction. Dogs do not bark at people's imaginations. No!" Holmes said, emphatically. "There was something or someone else here that night. If we can but flesh it out, we will be a step closer to bringing the guilty party or parties to justice."

We trudged a little way and, once again, found the two parallel lines in the snow running 'nor west to southeast. Obviously, the tracks of Hollis' sledge went from their cabin in the forest, to the inn that night.

"Do you see the thin tracks of the sledge with large footprint between them, Watson? This shows that Hollis was pulling both his daughter and the dog on the sledge. The trail runs uninterrupted until, at the point nearest the scene of the murder, the large footprints brake away and head off alone in that direction."

"Well, that agrees with Mr. Hollis' story so far." I commented.

"Right." Holmes agreed, moving a few more yards along the track. He pointed with his walking stick. "And at this point, we observe that some very large canine paw marks have replaced Hollis'. As indicated by the prints, the animal had begun to follow his master away from the sledge. Suddenly, the prints turn and head back to the sledge where they gather in an obviously frantic pattern. Aha!" Holmes exclaimed. "What's this then!?"

Another line of paw marks headed off in a 'nor easterly direction.

"Do you see how the paw marks are less defined and smeared Watson?"

I nodded that I agreed.

"The smearing reveals that the animal had been at a run and was probably chasing something.

"A squirrel or a hedgehog perhaps?" I offered.

"Not unless it was a flying squirrel one hears about. But I've never heard of a flying hedgehog. Whatever the dog had been chasing, it left no marks in the snow.

"A bird then?"

"From Hollis' description of the animal, Cromwell is too obedient to have jeopardized little Agnes' safety by indulging in anything as rash as chasing night fowl. The animal's marks stop a yard or two away and then turn back to the sledge once more."

All of this corroborated both Hollis and little Agnes' stories that Hollis had left his dog with the sledge and that, while Hollis was away, something had agitated the dog. Yet, as evidenced by the paw marks, Cromwell had stayed close to his charge.

CHAPTER NINE

I awoke the next morning, tired from our nocturnal excursion. I dressed, stopped at Holmes' room and knocked on the door. Receiving no answer, I went downstairs hoping to find him at breakfast. Holmes was nowhere to be found. I inquired at the desk and Mr. Pinkerton informed me that Holmes had arisen quit early and had left without eating. Mr. Pinkerton handed me a note from Holmes which read simply:

"Watson,
Have gone to Mall House asylum, will return after noon.
Young Pinkerton boy in poor health. Your expertise may be
of assistance.
SH"

I thanked Pinkerton, and inquired after his son.

Pinkerton shook his head and gestured in the direction of the stairs. "The boy awoke this morning complaining of the mullygrubs and grabbing at his belly. At first, I believed him to be only playing at Hookem-snivey so as to escape his chores, but he's vomited more than once this morning."

"I'll see to the boy gladly." I assured him.

I felt for the lad of course, yet I was also grateful for the work while Holmes was away. Colin Pinkerton was a toe-headed boy of eleven. He lay in his bed, pasty and sweating. After a quick examination, I found that the boy's "illness" was nothing more than (he admitted after some interrogation on my part) the natural effects of the lad and the other village youths having raided the inn's store of ale on the previous night.

"Well, I'll be frummag'd!" Exclaimed the innkeeper when I revealed the truth. "You mean that the boys have been getting bung-eyed on my ale? I'll tan his pratt! He'll not sit for a week!"

Having been a somewhat rambunctious youth once myself, I felt for the Pinkerton boy.

"As a medical man, may I suggest an even more effective prescription?"

"What would that be doctor?"

"Nothing makes a man sober up faster and cleaner than a full day of manual labor. Your wife has been good enough to teach Mr. Hollis' daughter her lessons. I'm sure that he would be glad to do you a turn by teaching your son his. The boy will be as clear-headed as a Friar by the afternoon."

Mr. Pinkerton's scowl slowly turned into a full grin from ear to ear. "You're a right evil schemer Doctor, do you know that?" Mr. Pinkerton laughed. "But I'm not sure I can convince the missus."

"Tell her it is the doctor's orders." I answered, laughing along.

I broke my fast on ham and eggs, cheese and a small loaf of bread. Mr. and Mrs. Pinkerton retired to their private quarters, I presumed to discuss their son's night-time activities as well as my suggestion. Presently, I discovered that my advice had been heeded when I saw young Pinkerton leave the inn, lunch tin in hand and heading north over The Scrubs in the general direction of Hollis' cabin. I chuckled to myself, remembering a young John Watson learning a similar lesson.

I passed the rest of the morning lazily wandering the streets and shops of Shepherd's Bush. I was struck by how the wonders of the industrial age and the traditions of the area's agrarian past intermingled. To the far south of the town and on into Hammersmith proper, there were large warehouses, workshops and factories. The northern parts of the area however, held steadfastly to a simpler way of life. I spent the day roaming the town and then returned to the inn just before dinner.

Near sundown, Holmes returned from his mission to the asylum. Upon arriving, he went to his room and changed into his evening clothes.

"In all, a productive day, Watson." He beamed over a plate of cold pheasant.

"Did you find anything pertinent?" I inquired.

"I must say that I have indeed."

"Don't keep me in suspense then, Holmes."

"If you recall Watson, upon our arrival at the prison yesterday, we were witness to the forceful transfer of the frantic and apparently mad convict to the asylum at Mall House.

"Yes, indeed." I agreed.

"You may also recall that Colonel Calhoun, the

Warden, indicated that it is not unusual for many of his newer prisoners to suffer the same fate."

I nodded.

"Also, if you remember, Calhoun named the man as one Alpheus Skinner; known in the criminal world of London as a master safe crack. Calhoun then expressed his surprise that this prisoner of over two years would behave in such a manner. As they dragged the incoherent man to the paddy wagon, I noticed that the man's bare chest and arms were sun tanned and as brown as a nut; completely inconsistent with someone who had been incarcerated within the dark cells of a London prison for the past three years. I also noticed two tattoo marks, one on each forearm, in the form of an anchor and a mermaid. I then expressed my disbelief to Colonel Calhoun, who took such offense at my question that I let the matter rest for the time being."

"Risking the chase of a wild goose, yet having reached an impasse in the case of the murdered guards, I left you at the inn this morning and paid a visit to the asylum to question this convict Skinner. When I arrived and introduced myself, the man nearly broke down and cried; so thankful was he that someone believed his story. At this meeting, in the visiting room of the asylum, he was a completely different man indeed. He seemed to be self-possessed and bore little resemblance to the lunatic that passed us the previous day. He was bathed, groomed and seemed very much of a sound mind. I asked him if his name was Alpheus Skinner. It was then that he repeated the words he had shouted the day before. 'I am not him.'

'I believe you sir.' I assured him. 'What is your name then?'

He seemed surprised at my acceptance of his claims and answered, 'My name is Danforth Skinner. Alpheus is the accursed demon with whom I shared the womb; he is my twin. I will no longer use the word 'brother' to speak of him.'

The scenario began to take shape in my mind and I asked how he came to be in Wormwood Scrubs prison in the place of Alpheus. He told me that since leaving home, he had always been a mariner. I nodded, remembering the tattoo marks. He stated that on his last voyage, he was signed aboard the merchant ship '*Marlborough*' which, if you recall, disappeared in January of this year. He admits that just prior to sailing, he deserted the ship at Lyttleton, New Zealand and did not board the ill-fated vessel as it sailed home for London; a decision he does not regret. Some weeks after the ship was reported missing, he was shocked and ashamed when he found his own name listed on the manifest as 'lost at sea'. He made his way by hook and crook back to London and, fearing imprisonment for desertion, made his existence known only to his brother Alpheus who was incarcerated at Wormwood Scrubs.

It seems that Alpheus' criminal syndicate, having need of his particular 'skills' as a safe cracker, seized upon the opportunity and devised a plan to break Alpheus out of prison and replace him with his 'deceased' twin brother Danforth.

'What is your recollection of the night you were abducted?' I asked.

'Since arriving in London, I have been living in squalor in a room above an opium den at the London docks, hoping that either rum or vice might soon put an end to my guilt and misery. Late on Halloween night, I staggered drunkenly into the dark streets. I remember the wharf being deserted and that I was completely alone. Suddenly, the already dark streets grew darker still, the shadows deepened and the darkness became palpable. I suddenly had the feeling that I was being followed. Being that it was Halloween, terrible yet nameless fears entered my rum soaked mind and I started running blindly back to my rooms. A few moments later, I felt a sharp blow to the top of my head, my lights went out and I remembered nothing more until I awoke on a cot in a prison cell. I had assumed that I had finally been arrested for jumping ship, until I realized that all the prison warders were referring to me as Alpheus. It was then that I understood what that monster that shares my face had done to me.'"

"That Watson," Holmes concluded with a flourish of his hand, "was essentially Mr. Skinner's account as he told it to me."

"Remarkable!" I exclaimed. "If you can prove this out and track this Alpheus, you will have saved a man's life."

"I have already sent Lestrade a description of the man and the hunt is under way."

Holmes smiled, devoured his bird and quickly changed the subject. "How went your day Watson? I trust the boy's ailment was alleviated by your skills?"

I narrated the story to Holmes who found it all novel, yet entertaining.

"The mischief of young boys," Holmes said, "is and will always be somewhat amusing, as long as they eventually outgrow that mischievousness. My 'bread and butter' however, is the result of mischievous little boys who have grown into criminal men."

"If Hollis does right by Mr. Pinkerton, the lad should be well on his way to amending his habits by now, I presume."

"Unless I miss my guess, we are about to witness those results now." Holmes said, indicating the now opening door.

I followed Holmes' gaze and saw Hollis, Agnes and young Pinkerton just entering the inn. Every observable movement of the boy's body gave testimony to Hollis' fulfillment of the favor. The young boy's clothes were filthy, his body drooped and the bandages covering his hands spoke of unseen blisters. His penitent face was downcast as he stood before the giant. Hollis sent little Agnes upstairs with a pat.

"May I go now too, Sir?" The lad pleaded humbly.

"Aye. Off with you lad and I trust that you've learned your lesson and won't be coming to visit me again anytime soon?"

"No sir. I won't."

"And remember." Hollis said in a softer tone, while handing the boy his lunch tin. "A man is judged by the character of his companions as much as he is his own."

"Yes Sir." The boy said, his feet dragging the floor as he made his way across the room and up the stairs.

As soon as the boy was out of sight, Hollis gave a loud, yet good-hearted laugh, hung up his axe and made his way over to the bar. A roguish smile as wide as his face beamed out from under his copious beard as he sauntered passed us.

Presently, Mr. Pinkerton came down the stairs,

chuckling and smiling. Upon seeing Hollis, he went to the bar, poured four pints and motioned Holmes and I over. "The drinks are on the house tonight, gentlemen. I thank you for your help with the boy today." He said to both Hollis and me.

"Think nothing of it." We both answered, in unison.

"I'm glad I could help in some small way." Hollis added.

"Not such a small way to be sure Bill." Pinkerton said. "I do believe that boy is so tuckered, he may just join '*The Sons of Temperance*', tee-totaling movement first thing tomorrow.

We all laughed as Hollis raised his tankard. "To the lessons of youth!" He proposed.

"To the lessons of youth!" We all echoed and clanked our mugs together in a toast.

We drank and smoked a while as the fire roared in the hearth and we regaled each other with similar tales from our own pasts.

"I just wonder," I mused, "if the punishment was equal to a few stolen pints of ale."

Hollis shook his massive head. "Not so doctor. It was more than just a few pints, and it wasn't only last night, I'm sure."

"What makes you say that, Mr. Hollis?" I inquired.

"Earlier, as I was walking him home, the lad confided to me that he and his chums had gotten so blithered on Halloween night, that they began to have visions of flying packy derms."

Everyone laughed except Holmes, who jolted and leaned forward. "Would you please repeat that, Mr. Hollis?"

"The boy told me that they were so drunk, they imagined seeing an elephant soaring across The Scrubs that night."

"That's it, Watson!" Holmes shouted, banged his fist on the table and shot to his feet. "How could I have been so blind? Mr. Pinkerton I must see your son immediately."

But Mr. Holmes," Pinkerton protested, "the boy is plumb done in and is sure to be already asleep."

"I really must insist. It is most urgent." Holmes

maintained.

Pinkerton shook his head in resignation and turned toward his apartments.

"Also, if you have a map of the area it would be helpful." Holmes added.

Pinkerton pointed behind the bar. "In the drawer under the counter." He said, and went to fetch the boy as Holmes paced restlessly before the fire. I found the map (*the very one that I have provided. jhw*) and brought it back to the table. A few moments later, the boy followed his father down and then stood, at the foot of the stairs, rubbing his eyes sleepily.

"My apologies to you Master Pinkerton, but I have a few questions that only you can answer." Holmes said, motioning the lad over and offering him a glass of water. "Here drink this down. This will only take a few moments, I promise."

Holmes unfolded the map onto the table and then, looking at the boy, said, "Alright Colin, can you please indicate here on the map, where you and your chums were on Halloween night?"

The boy studied the map a moment and then pointed to a group of buildings just northwest of the inn.

"There." He said. "We were sitting on the bluff behind the Old Oak Farm."

"Now, can you show us where you saw the 'flying elephant'?"

The boy pointed to the map at exactly the location of the first murder.

"Splendid!" Holmes exclaimed. "Now, Colin. I need for you to consider the next question carefully."

Colin nodded.

"Good boy." Holmes said. "Can you show me the *direction* in which the 'elephant' was flying?"

Again, Colin studied the map, laid a finger on the previous spot and then moved it in a 'nor easterly direction.

"Capital!" Holmes exclaimed, patting the lad on the back. "Just as I might have suspected!"

"One last question, if you please. Did the 'elephant' light up the sky and make a sound?"

Colin looked puzzled at Holmes.

"Did the thing light up like a lantern?" Holmes

urged.

"No Sir, it was as black as the night and silent as a ghost."

Obviously expecting different answers, Holmes looked puzzled himself. "No lights or sound at all? Are you certain of this Colin?"

"Yes Sir. We probably would have missed it, but it blocked out the stars as it went."

Holmes stood up and clapped the lad on the back. "Thank you Colin, you have been most helpful indeed. Now, off to bed with you; and may the remainder of your rest be undisturbed."

The boy looked to his father who also patted the boy on the back and nodded. "Good night son." Pinkerton said. "Sleep well."

Colin turned and made his way back upstairs.

Holmes bent over the map once again. After studying it for a moment, he traced his finger along the same trajectory Colin had indicated. Following a 'nor easterly route, Holmes' finger rested on a small grouping of buildings in the upper left-hand quadrant of the map.

"Mr. Pinkerton, what can you tell me of these structures?" Holmes inquired.

Pinkerton squinted over the map a moment. "That there is the 'Red House Farm', Mr. Holmes.

"Who lives there?"

"No one." Pinkerton asserted. "It's been allowed to go to seed, you might say, since old man Riley passed ten year ago."

Holmes took out his glass and studied the specific area of the map. "I see here, that there are two structures. I assume the larger one is the house?"

"On the contrary Mr. Holmes." Pinkerton said, laying a finger on the smaller of the two rectangles. "This one is the house. The barn there is larger than the house is."

"How much larger?"

Pinkerton considered the question and then finally said, "At least twice a long and double the height."

"And why would the farm need such a large barn?" Holmes wondered aloud.

"Sheep's the thing 'round these parts, of course. A

proper farm needs a place to store feed as well as the wool before marketing. The shepherds around here also use it as an auction-house on occasion."

"Is the property vacant then?"

"There was a group of local rugby players that used the plot for practice a while back, but they moved first to 'The Pavilion' south of there and then away all together. The place is, as far as I know, completely deserted now."

Holmes stood and began folding the map into his pocket. "I believe," he said, "that a visit to this farm is in order, Watson. Mr. Pinkerton, is your horse and wagon available?"

"Yes, but I'll not bother the boy again to hitch the trap."

"I wouldn't hear of it." Holmes assured him. "We can take care of that ourselves, of course. Eh Watson?"

"Indeed. By all means, let the boy sleep." I agreed.

CHAPTER TEN

We made quick work of preparing the wagon and in fifteen minutes we were rattling northward on Wood Lane toward Red House Farm. There was no moon and the darkness of the night necessitated the use of the lanterns in order to navigate the well rutted road. When we had gotten as far as 'The Rifle Pavilion', Holmes reigned in the trap behind an outbuilding in the rear of the structure. From there, we began to walk the remaining distance, carrying only one of the lanterns for safety's sake.

As we approached a low stone wall that marked the perimeter of Red House Farm, Holmes shut the lantern and motioned for me to follow silently. We scaled the wall and advanced upon the house first; to ensure that it was indeed vacant. The house was painted in a deep crimson colour befitting its name, although as evidenced by the faded and peeling paint; it had not been retouched in some considerable time. Holmes and I peeped into a large bay window at the front of the home. Seeing no lights inside, Holmes ventured to open the lantern just a sliver, and shined it into the room. Pinkerton had been correct. As we surveyed the room beyond, we discovered that it was absolutely devoid of any furnishings or signs of habitation.

Holmes reclosed the lantern and indicated that we move on to the barn next. Again, true to Pinkerton's word, the barn was at least twice as long and double the height of the house. It was painted the same blood red as the house and had a row of small windows running just under the eaves on the two longer sides of the building. At either end of the building, there were two enormous sliding doors that stretched from the ground to the roof some twenty feet high. This time, Holmes chose a roundabout approach to the barn. I followed him as he made a wide circuit around the structure.

As we came around the north side of the barn, Holmes suddenly lost his footing and very nearly fell. I looked ahead and saw that Holmes had tripped over what I initially took to be a low fence. Upon closer inspection, I saw that it was a run of piping that ran out of the northern wall of the barn and continued northward off into the distance. We climbed over them and continued around to the rear of the barn. As we reached the eastern side, we noticed a small copse of trees some fifty yards away. We made for the shadows beneath them and waited. From my vantage point, there was nothing to indicate that the barn was any less vacant than the house had been.

Holmes tipped his head toward mine and whispered. "As we were going around the front, I took notice of several tracks in the snow, going in and out of the big front door. The barn, at least, does not seem as vacant as did the house, Watson."

"Do you think that those who made the tracks are inside?"

"To know that, we must wait here a while and observe. Keep your eyes and ears sharp for any human sounds Watson; voices, snoring or the like."

After ten minutes, having neither seen nor heard anything except the occasional bleating of a distant herd of sheep, Holmes and I made our way toward the dark building. Upon reaching the side opposite the road, we crouched down and pressed ourselves against the side of the barn. Again, we listened for a few moments for any sign of habitation. Still hearing nothing but the normal sounds of the night, we were emboldened to attempt entry through the large doors on the South end. Just prior to entering, I drew my revolver.

Once inside, Holmes lit the lamp. The cavernous interior was untenanted, yet far from empty. As soon as my eyes adjusted, I saw in one corner, five cots, a table with a deck of cards and a makeshift kitchen. Curiously, along the western wall, there were as many as fifty milk canisters, all stacked neatly on shelves. Along the opposite wall, there were a number of pallets loaded with what looked like leather swatches the size of hearth rugs. These were bundled and stacked up almost to the ceiling. After closer inspection, my medical eye told me that they were sheep's stomachs that had been flattened and stretched.

By far the most gruesome discovery came when I searched the corner near the card table. I startled when on a row of shelves, I saw two large jars, each filled with a disembodied head in some sort of clear liquid. They had obviously been put on display by the villains as macabre trophies.

"We seem to have found both Jenkins and Baldwin." I guessed.

I replaced the grisly things and surveyed the rest of the barn. Finally, down at the other side of the warehouse almost blocking the large barn doors, I saw what at first I took to be a junk pile. To my eye, it reminded me of some descriptions I had read of 'stills' that the hillbillies of the Appalachian mountains in America are known to use to distill corn spirits. The apparatus consisted of a jumble of copper tubing, bladders, a bellows, a large coal bin and two metal tanks. Seeing it, I was also reminded of the chemistry equipment in both Professor Ramsay's laboratory as well as Holmes' work table at Baker Street.

"Do you see Watson?" Holmes said, obviously impressed. "Unless my knowledge of shepherding is much flawed, this is a far larger operation than I had originally conceived."

"What do you think it is Holmes?"

Holmes studied the contraption further. His eyes finally fell upon the shelving that held the milk canisters. "Unless I miss my guess, the answer is to be found in those milk canisters, which they have obviously been using as storage and shipping containers."

"Storage of what cargo do you wonder?" I pondered aloud.

"Again, my knowledge of shepherding may be lacking, but I do not think that the market for sheep's milk would justify this number of milk containers."

Holmes walked over to the nearest shelf and dragged out one of the canisters. In the dim light of the lantern, I took note that the canisters had been modified and on the lids of each one, there had been installed some sort of spigot. Holmes bent down and opened the spigot a turn.

A hissing sound which startled us both erupted from the valve.

"By Jove Holmes!" I exclaimed. "Who would have ever conceived of such a thing? Converting milk canisters for...." I paused, my words failing me. "For what purpose, Holmes" I questioned.

"There is true genius at work here Watson." Holmes said. He sniffed the air and thought a moment. "Do you recall the pipes outside the barn, which we were forced to climb over?"

"Yes, my leg wound remembers them quite well." I replied.

Holmes removed Pinkerton's map and held it under the lamplight. He pointed to a group of circular structures just north and slightly west of Red House Farm.

"See here Watson! The gas works! By Jove! Those pipes are tapped into the gas works, or I'm not worth my salt. These are no mere cut-throats or pickpockets. This is a black business to be sure. But why would they want to tap the London gas works?"

"A bomb perhaps?" I suggested.

"It is possible." Holmes agreed, but not without a look of reservation showing on his face. He sniffed at the air again. "Watson, do you detect the smell of gas in this room?"

I smelled the air. "Not a trace of it Holmes."

"Right! There should be a distinct scent of either ammonia or sulfur."

I pointed to the milk canisters. "Perhaps it is merely compressed air then?"

Holmes extinguished the lantern, bent his face toward the spigot and drew in a long breath. Sensing danger, I reached out to stop him.

Holmes staved me off with his own hand. He sniffed the air again and then stood up. "No worries Wats….." He stopped, stunned, because his voice had taken on a much higher-pitched tone.

"What is this madness Holmes?" I said. In spite of my concern for Holmes' health, I found myself chuckling at the outlandish sound of his voice.

"I do not yet know, Watson." He said; his voice still in a strange falsetto. "This is a strange marvel indeed." As he said this, his voice quickly deepened and returned to its normal tenor.

His face took on an indignant air as he recovered his composure. "This is no time for laughter Watson. Please control yourself. These men are a dangerous lot and we may have need of Scotland Yard before the night is over. Let us away from here and find Sergeant Quinn before they return."

The thought sobered me immediately and we made

our way back to the door through which we had entered. We began to make our way through the darkness; unwilling to relight the lantern lest the gang returned to their lair. As we slipped out into the night, I realized that without the lantern's light we would have some difficulty finding our way back to our wagon. Remembering my army training in celestial navigation, I sought to consult the stars for orientation. As I looked skyward, I stood confused and astonished, seeing only black sky where only minutes before there had been a starlit night. It took a moment for my mind to register the fact that the stars were not missing; they were being blocked, by some massive and silent shape some thirty feet above our heads.

"Watson!" Holmes shouted. "Make for cove…." His voice was abruptly cut off.

Suddenly, I saw Holmes' entire body lift off the ground; his feet flailing wildly as he flew off southward. I drew my revolver and started firing at the black monster that had a rope around Holmes' throat. As I aimed, the shape of the thing began to reveal itself. It looked to me to be a balloon the shape of a bloated grain silo turned onto its side with a large basket hanging from underneath. I heard men's voices shouting curses back at me as I emptied my revolver into the thing. I hit my mark and one man fell from the basket to the snow below, but on the balloon itself, my bullets were having no affect whatever. As the craft continued to move southward away from the barn, I began to seriously despair of my friend's life.

Panic gripped me suddenly and I ran blindly after the quickly retreating figure of Holmes.

"Holmes!" I shouted in vain. "God help me! Holmes!"

Through the fear induced haze of my mind, I perceived a steady 'thump thump thump' sound from somewhere behind and above me. I looked upward toward the barn and saw another dark shape running quickly along the ridge line of the barn's rooftop. As I stood amazed, I saw the giant form of Hollis the woodsman leap from the barn some ten feet through the air with a roar as if from some Norse folktale; his massive ax bolting toward the craft as if it had been fired from a ballista. The deadly projectile sliced into the skin of the balloon, opening a gash large enough for a man to walk through. Hollis meanwhile had clinched the edge of the basket and was hauling himself up among the ship's crew.

The terror filled screams of the criminals could not have been more clamorous had the ghost of Blackbeard himself boarded their ship. I saw two of the men abandon ship in fright and jump the twenty feet to the ground. I heard their legs snap upon impact. Another of the gang had stood to challenge Hollis with some sort of unknown bladed weapon flashing in his hands. Hollis dodged the attack nimbly, grabbed the ruffian by the neck and hurled both he and the blade overboard after his comrades.

The craft continued heading southward while descending quickly; hissing and squealing like some wounded animal. I gave chase. The craft was now within twenty feet of the ground. This allowed me to catch up to Holmes and position myself beneath him. I grabbed his legs and lifted his body to loosen the tension of the rope. As his feet finally touched ground, I laid him down and began grabbing at the noose. Cursing my trembling hands, I could not free Holmes' neck. The still moving balloon began to drag Holmes' lifeless body along the ground. Looking around me in desperation, I spied a few yards distant, a large scythe that the fourth ruffian had lost as Hollis had tossed him from the ship. I ran, snatched up the deadly thing and dashed after Holmes. With a well-placed chop, I severed the line from the balloon. I returned to Holmes' side, and with surgeon's hands, I carefully began slicing through the rope. As the last strand broke free, I thankfully heard Holmes take a deep draught of air into his lungs.

He began hacking and coughing as life returned to his face.

"Thank God!" I exclaimed under my breath. I tried to restrain Holmes from moving unnecessarily lest there were any unseen injuries to his cervical vertebrae.

I looked back toward the airship and saw Hollis jump unharmed, from the craft just as it dove into the frozen ground with a thunderous crash. As the resulting flurry of snow began to settle, I heard another noise behind me. I reclaimed the scythe, stood and turned; ready to face any threat. When I recognized Sergeant Quinn, I lowered the weapon. He was accompanied by three other constables who were already rounding up the wounded criminals.

"Is he alright doctor?" Quinn asked, pointing to my friend.

I nodded and dropped the sickle. "Yes, but he needs a hospital. Our wagon is behind the rifle pavilion."

Quinn sent one of his men to retrieve the wagon and then assisted me in lifting Holmes into the bed. As we did so, I saw Hollis striding up. The giant was dragging two more criminals, both of them unconscious, behind him as he would have two tree branches.

"Just clearing out the bracken Constable." He said with a laugh as he deposited the two men at Quinn's feet.

As we drove off down Wood lane, I glanced back toward the crash site. The horrid thing lay deflating, in a mangled and twisted heap where it had landed near the stables on a short side road just eastward of the prison that, to this day, is known by the local inhabitants as 'Woodsman's Mews' in honor of the heroic lumberjack.

CHAPTER ELEVEN

I spent the next two days in hospital, caring for Holmes. It is a credit to his physical resilience that, on the third day, we were back at Baker Street where Mrs. Hudson fastidiously replaced me in the roll of nursemaid. Excluding myself, Holmes could want of no better care and by day's end, was nearly his old self. As Holmes reclined on the settee and I in my chair opposite him, there came a frantic banging at the door. I jumped up and opened it. As I did so, Inspector Lestrade fairly dove into the room attempting to escape Mrs. Hudson's maternal wrath in the form of an umbrella she'd found at the foot of the stairs.

"I told him that Mr. Holmes was in no condition to receive visitors Dr. Watson." She fairly shouted.

Holmes rose from his couch and in a raspy, gritty voice said, "It is quite alright Mrs. Hudson. I have wanted to speak with the Inspector for some time now."

Mrs. Hudson gave Lestrade one last whack with the umbrella, turned and left in a huff. As the door closed behind her, Lestrade attempted to recover some of his pride.

"I would be doing my duty to have that woman in the dock for assaulting an officer of Her Majesty's police!" He shouted, pointing at the door after her.

"I am afraid that you would lose that case Inspector, for I would be the loudest witness in her defense." Holmes chuckled, and then grabbed at his neck in pain.

I helped Holmes back to his seat. Lestrade took a chair by the fire, all the while mumbling something about 'duty', 'justice' and 'respect'.

Getting right down to the business at hand, Lestrade took a note pad and pencil from his vest pocket. "Now Mr. Holmes," He said, "If you are ready to give an official report of the Wormwood Scrubs business."

Holmes fluffed a pillow and placed it behind his head. "Of course Inspector, but I must insist that I be given liberty to tell the narrative in the way that I see fit; without any undue interrupting questions."

"As you wish." Lestrade agreed with an impatient wave of his hand.

Holmes cleared his damaged throat and began in a raspy voice. "I will begin on the day that we arrived at the scene of the first murder. As you recall, the body of Jenkins lay in an open, snow covered field with only his own tracks evident for some distance in any direction. It was this inscrutability that first interested me in the case. While surveying the location, I attempted to ascertain from whence the attack had come. I applied my old axiom, 'Once you eliminate the impossible, whatever remains, no matter how improbable, must be the truth".

Having eliminated an attack from North, South, East or West, I considered the two other spatial directions. Up and down. Down could be ruled out immediately, which left only one direction; up. You will remember that I lay in the impression left by the body in the snow. As I lay there, I immediately considered a hot air balloon. Laying that aside for the time being, I circumnavigated the entire location and found minuscule drops of blood heading off in a northeasterly direction. Upon examining the second site, where Baldwin met his demise, I found similar droplets trailing off in the same northeasterly direction. Sadly, in both cases, the trails ceased after some little distance.

Back at the inn that evening, my mind returned to the possibility of an attack by hot air balloon. Knowing that hot air balloons are both noisy and bright, I then questioned both Hollis and little Agnes as to whether they had seen or heard anything strange that night. Receiving a negative answer, (other than little Agnes' fairy voices) I was forced to rule out a hot air balloon. Yet, taking into consideration Agnes' testimony that she had heard fairies passing her overhead, as well as the dog Cromwell's apparent pursuit of 'night fowl'; I could not yet rule out an aerial attack.

It was not until after my visit to the asylum that I realized that the bodies of the two guards were ancillary crimes and not the principal crime at all.

"Not the principal crime? What then would you call two headless corpses Mr. Holmes?" Lestrade challenged.

"Retribution, Inspector. The tying up of loose ends, if you will." Holmes countered.

"So what was the 'principal crime' then?" Lestrade asked.

"A prison escape Inspector." Holmes answered curtly.

At this point in his narrative, Holmes arose, went to the fireplace and refilled his pipe from the Persian slipper. After lighting it and puffing a few smoke rings into the air, he began to pace back and forth upon the hearth.

"It had become clear to me," he continued, "that Danforth Skinner had somehow materialized within the walls of the prison; though an explanation of how such a thing could have been done under the noses of the prison supervision was not yet within my grasp. Obviously, the gang would have need of someone inside the prison to help them make the switch. It was then that I remembered the two dead guards; Jenkins and Baldwin. According to Mr. Teague's testimony, both Jenkins and Baldwin were in need of money and similarly, both seemed to have had very recent monetary windfalls; neither of which carried an explanation as to the origin of the newly acquired funds. It is my belief that the two of them, being morally compromised, were propositioned by Alpheus Skinner to assist in his escape. I have no doubt that Alpheus' assurance that a replacement prisoner would be provided and therefore no empty cell was a deciding factor in turning the two men traitor.   No empty cell, no escape. Satisfied, both Jenkins and Baldwin took the bribes, and having either outlived their usefulness or having become liabilities to the syndicate, had paid the ultimate price for their treason.

In the cases of both Danforth Skinner's mysterious appearance in the prison as well as the beheadings of the two guards, there seemed to be a common thread. According to Mr. Teague's account, on Halloween night, he heard what he called 'the screech of the banshee' from above him in the dark night sky.   Little Agnes asserted that she heard 'fairy voices' and 'wings flapping' above her, as well as the dog Cromwell's chasing an unseen thing in the sky.   Also, Danforth Skinner could not have been dragged unconscious over the walls of the prison or carried through the front gate without being seen and his brother Alpheus could not have scaled the walls or just walked through the front gate of the prison.   All of these things led my focus skyward and suggested that the both the prison escape and the murders were somehow linked.

Remember that at the murder scenes out on The Scrubs, I had eliminated an attack from North, South, East, West and down, and settled on up; so too I deduced that Alpheus Skinner had traded places with his brother by taking to the air. Finally, when I heard of young Pinkerton's ostensibly ale induced visions of a flying 'elephant' over The Scrubs on Halloween night, I was sure that some sort of balloon, though not of the hot air variety, had been used in both cases."

"Impossible! How could the criminals take to the air in a balloon without using hot air to do it?" Lestrade challenged.

Holmes continued patiently. "On the day of our visit to the prison, we made an examination of the corpses of both victims where we serendipitously found the note in Jenkins's shoe. This was the first solid lead in the case. The note made mention of a 'Ramsay at University College' whom we visited later that day."

Making a note in his pad, Lestrade said, "I'll have a warrant to bring this Ramsay in for questioning then."

"Never mind that Inspector, Ramsay is innocent and was completely uninvolved." Holmes assured him.

Lestrade held up his finger in protest. "But if this Professor Ramsay was not in league with the criminals, why did their note say that 'he would do the job nicely'?"

"Alas!" Holmes exclaimed with an air of self-admonition. "That is the point where I missed the mark completely."

At this confession, Lestrade fairly giggled with delight.

Holmes ignored the slight, knocked the ashes from his pipe into the fireplace and continued. "The reference to Professor Ramsay in the note was not, as he assumed, an allusion to the 'gold from sea-water' venture, but to his ongoing research of the noble gases for which he is so famous."

"I don't follow." Lestrade said with a shake of his head.

"I'm afraid that I too am at a loss." I admitted.

The word 'He' in the note was not referring to Ramsay at all, but to one of his most recent discoveries.

The letters 'He' are the designation given to the elemental gas 'Helium' in Mendeleev's periodic table. The intended message was therefore, that Helium would 'do the job nicely'. The 'job' of course, being to hoist the balloon whilst giving off neither light nor sound as the conventional hot air variety would most certainly have done; thus giving the gang the advantage of stealth.

Yesterday in hospital, while you were out Watson, I was visited by Professor Ramsay and he furnished me with a few missing strands of the web. Firstly, he informed me that Helium, being far lighter than air, would indeed 'do the job' of lifting the flying machine and Alpheus over the walls of the prison. It also has the strange side effect, as you will remember Watson, of changing the timbre of one's voice when inhaled; thus explaining little Agnes's 'fairy voices'.

I chuckled at the recollection.

"But how could the Helium have affected the crew of the balloon in such a way?" I wondered.

"As they flew over the walls of the prison, they came within earshot of Warder Teague if you remember.

The unearthly shrieking noise that he took to be a banshee tells us that the balloon must have been suffering a slow leak; a leak of Helium that had caused their voices to rise in pitch to fairy-like squeaks by the time they flew over little Agnes and the dog Cromwell out on The Scrubs.

The Professor also explained the reason for the other two names mentioned in the note.

"Who are they?" Lestrade asked.

"Professor Ramsay explained that, only yesterday morning, he recalled that in 1869, Sir Norman Lockyer, along with a French astronomer named Pierre Jansenn, had discovered a new element around the corona of the eclipsed sun that they named 'Helium' after the Greek sun god Helios. Up until now, Helium was believed only to exist in outer space. It is at this point where Ramsay realized the reason for his name being on the note. He himself has only very recently discovered that Helium can indeed be found on Earth. The discovery is so recent in fact, that he has not yet even published a paper on his findings. The mastermind behind this crime somehow learned of Ramsay's work and that Helium could be obtained by purifying common household gas. The contraption in the barn at the Red House Farm was designed to distill the Helium from the gas that they had syphoned from the London gas works just north of the farm."

"And then stored it in the milk containers until needed to fill the balloon?" I interjected.

"Precisely, Watson." Holmes agreed.

"But what of the other name, 'Kober'? Lestrade asked.

"Ah yes," Said Holmes, "On that point Ramsay shows promise as a detective. With a little research on his part, he found that Theodore Kober is a promising engineer working for a German balloon manufacturer. It was one of Kober's designs that the criminal syndicate had stolen and used to build their craft. They lacked the silk that is commonly used in such vessels and were forced to sew together the sheep's stomachs that we saw stored in the barn."

"Well," said Lestrade as he rose and fetched his hat and coat, "you certainly have made a job for me to nab this Alpheus Skinner and to write this all into some kind of coherent report to The Yard."

"Both of which I am sure you will accomplish with haste and proficiency Inspector." Holmes encouraged.

After Lestrade left, Holmes and I once again sat in front of the fire at 221b Baker Street, smoking a last pipe in silence before I had to return to my own hearth and to Mary. As I was getting up to leave, Mrs. Hudson entered and delivered a telegram. Holmes read it and then passed it to me.

"It seems," he said, "that my brother Mycroft, with the help of his contacts in the British government, has secured for Mr. Hollis our woodsman savior, a Royal commendation in the form of a land grant and a yearly income of £120 to prune, tend and clear Her Majesty's woodlands in upper Hammersmith."

"Huzzah! Jolly good for him. They'll not want for much from now on." I exclaimed, rising from my chair.

"Here here!" Holmes agreed. "Also, due to the particular atmospheric conditions at Wormwood Scrubs demonstrated by the criminal's balloon, Mycroft has submitted to The Admiralty, a plan to begin building and testing such flying balloons there in future."

"It certainly seems an ideal place for such a thing, and a poetic justice of sorts as well." I commented.

As I turned and opened the door to leave, I heard Holmes give a chuckle.

"Did you say something Holmes?" I asked.

He stood by the mantle, gazing wistfully into the fire. "I was just contemplating."

"What upon Holmes?" I urged.

"It has only just occurred to me, that the solution to this case in particular was indeed; '*Element*'ary my dear Watson, Elementary."

The End

Also From MX Publishing

Winners of the 2011 Howlett Literary Award (Sherlock Holmes book of the year) for 'The Norwood Author'

From one of the world's largest Sherlock Holmes publishers dozens of new novels from the top Holmes authors around the world.

www.mxpublishing.com

Including our bestselling short story collections 'Lost Stories of Sherlock Holmes' and 'The Outstanding Mysteries of Sherlock Holmes'.

New in 2012 [Novels unless stated]:

Sherlock Holmes and the Plague of Dracula
Sherlock Holmes and The Adventure of The Jacobite Rose [Play]
Sherlock Holmes and The Whitechapel Vampire
Holmes Sweet Holmes
The Detective and The Woman: A Novel of Sherlock Holmes
Sherlock Holmes Tales From The Stranger's Room
The Sherlock Holmes Who's Who
Sherlock Holmes and The Dead Boer at Scotney Castle
A Professor Reflects on Sherlock Holmes [Essay Collection]
Sherlock Holmes of The Lyme Regis Legacy
Sherlock Holmes and The Discarded Cigarette [Short Novel]
Sherlock Holmes On The Air [Radio Plays]
Sherlock Holmes and The Murder at Lodore Falls

David Ruffle

 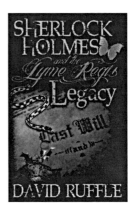

Sherlock Holmes and The Lyme Regis Horror and the sequel
Sherlock Holmes and The Lyme Regis Legacy

Sherlock Holmes – Tales from the Stranger's Room
An eclectic collection of writings from twenty Holmes writers.

www.mxpublishing.com

Also from MX Publishing

Sherlock Holmes Travel Guides

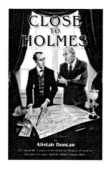

And in ebook (stunning on the iPad) an interactive guide

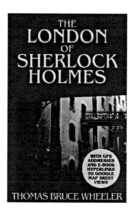

400 locations linked to Google Street View.

  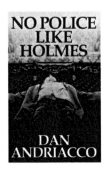

Short fiction (Discarded Cigarette, Russian Chessboard),
modern novels (No Police Like Holmes), a female Sherlock
Holmes (My Dear Watson) and the adventures of Mrs Watson
(Sign of Fear, and Study in Crimson).

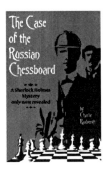  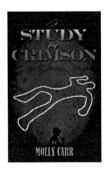

Also from MX Publishing

Biographies of Arthur Conan Doyle

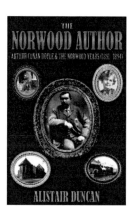 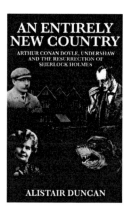

The Norwood Author. Winner of the 2011 Howlett Literary
Award (Sherlock Holmes Book of the year) and the most
important historical Holmes book of 2012 'An Entirely New
Country'

Also from MX Publishing

Cross over fiction featuring great villans from history

and military history Holmes thrillers

 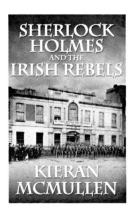

Also from MX Publishing

Fantasy Sherlock Holmes

And epic novels

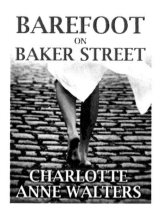

Lightning Source UK Ltd.
Milton Keynes UK
UKOW05f1006281013

219918UK00001B/8/P